"The girl you once knew no longer exists."

Francesca took one step back. "Except, perhaps, in your overheated imagination. And... and you don't seem to have the first idea about the woman she's become!"

"Then maybe it's time I began finding out," he drawled mockingly, his green eyes glinting with intent as he pulled her closer to his tall, muscular figure.

"What are you trying to prove? I...I don't feel anything for you. Not now...!" she panted breathlessly.

"Don't you?" he murmured as his dark head came down toward her.

MARY LYONS is happily married to an Essex farmer, has two children and lives in an old Victorian rectory. Life is peaceful—unlike her earlier years when she worked as a radio announcer, reviewed books and even ran for parliament in a London dockland area. She still loves a little excitement and combines romance with action and suspense in her books whenever possible.

Books by Mary Lyons

Don't miss any of our special offers. Write to us at the following address for information on our newest releases.

Harlequin Reader Service
P.O. Box 1397, Buffalo, NY 14240
Canadian address: P.O. Box 603,
Fort Erie, Ont. L2A 5X3

MARY LYONS

Silver Lady

Harlequin Books

TORONTO • NEW YORK • LONDON
AMSTERDAM • PARIS • SYDNEY • HAMBURG
STOCKHOLM • ATHENS • TOKYO • MILAN
MADRID • WARSAW • BUDAPEST • AUCKLAND

ISBN 0-373-11610-1

SILVER LADY

Copyright © 1991 by Mary Lyons.

This edition published by arrangement with Harlequin Enterprises B. V.

® and TM are trademarks of the publisher. Trademarks indicated with
® are registered in the United States Patent and Trademark Office, the
Canadian Trade Marks Office and in other countries.

Printed in U.S.A.

CHAPTER ONE

MOONLIGHT poured in through the open window of the bedroom, clearly illuminating the man as he walked slowly and silently towards her. Tall, dark-haired and sensationally handsome, he exuded a forceful air of power and strength as he drew close to her trembling figure.

Unable to move, paralysed by the gleam in his emerald-green eyes set beneath heavy eyelids, she stared helplessly up at the man, who—apart from a short white towel tied about his slim hips—was clearly naked.

The shafts of silver moonlight cutting through the dark, shadowy room seemed to magnify his height and the width of his broad shoulders; the deep tan of his skin was glistening with tiny droplets of water from a recent shower.

As he raised his hands to her bare shoulders, she shivered and trembled at the sensual, erotic touch of his fingers against her heated flesh.

'Francesca. . .?'

She couldn't speak. It seemed as if time and space had ceased to exist. She was caught up in a spell—a need and desire so intense that she was hardly aware of her pounding heartbeat.

'Francesca. . .?'

'Oh, yes—*yes!*' she whispered, finding her voice at

5

last and almost swooning in a roaring tide of passion and ecstasy. There was a deep ringing in her ears as he lowered his dark head, until his mouth was only an inch or two away from her own quivering lips.

'Francesca. . .?' he breathed softly. '*Why don't you answer the telephone*?'

'W-what. . .?'

Francesca Patterson woke with a start, her dazed mind desperately trying to cling on to the reality of her dream. But it was swiftly evaporating, dissolving and fading away in the face of the imperative, urgent summons from the instrument beside her bed.

She put out an arm, her hand flailing helplessly around until her fingers came into contact with the telephone.

'Y-yes. . .? Who is it?' she mumbled.

'Good morning. This is your alarm call, Miss Patterson,' a cheerful voice announced. 'Have a nice day!'

Francesca struggled to sit up, replacing the receiver and blinkling groggily down at her wrist-watch, before pushing a tired hand through her long ash-blonde hair.

Some of her friends seemed to think nothing of flying across the Atlantic for a weekend in New York. However, she'd always been badly affected by jet lag, and after yesterday's long flight to the Caribbean island of Grenada—not to mention the lengthy, tedious amount of time spent in the airport terminals—she'd have willingly given everything she possessed to be able to go back to sleep again. However, it was now eight o'clock. If she was to be at Prickly Bay by ten, she had no alternative but to get up and get dressed, as quickly as possible.

At the reminder of this morning's appointment, a deep flush spread across her pale cheeks. Quickly tossing aside the light sheet and swinging her legs off the bed, she padded across the cool marble floor towards the hotel room's large en-suite bathroom.

After cleaning her teeth and splashing her face with cold water, Francesca raised her head from the towel to stare dismally at her reflection in the mirror. The normally clear, brilliant aquamarine-blue eyes set below a high, wide brow were now misty and clouded with guilt and nervous apprehension.

It was years since she'd been tormented by that shadowy erotic dream which had repeatedly plagued her late teens. She was now twenty-four, she told herself firmly. A successful businesswoman, who had long ago put aside such childish fantasies. So—what on earth had come over her? How *could* she be so foolish as to still be dreaming about Matt like that. . .?

Squirming with shame and embarrassment, she quickly tossed aside the towel. Walking back through the bedroom, she pulled aside the flimsy curtains before opening the wooden louvred french doors and stepping out on to a shady patio overlooking Grand Anse Beach.

As she gazed across the shimmering golden sand towards the blue Caribbean Sea, it seemed incredible to recall that it had been snowing when she'd left London yesterday. It certainly looked as if it was going to be yet another scorchingly hot day in paradise, she told herself wryly, noting that the fiery ball of the sun had already risen well over the horizon, the muted roar of the waves beating on the shore seeming to echo the turbulent confusion in her tired brain.

It was three years since she'd last seen her stepbrother Matthew Sinclair. And she certainly wouldn't be here now if it hadn't been a matter of such vital importance. Goodness knows, Matt had made it difficult enough for her to contact him. It had taken weeks of persistent phone calls to the New York office of Sinclair International before she'd grudgingly been given the information that he was on vacation, sailing around the Caribbean. And it had taken even longer to persuade his chief assistant to arrange today's meeting.

To anyone who didn't know Matt it would seem quite ridiculous of her to be in such a state of nerves about meeting him. However, those who had anything to do with Wall Street, or the City of London, could tell a different story. 'Sinclair Strikes Again' had been a frequent newspaper headline over the past few years as many companies—and even well-established corporate institutions—had allowed themselves to be taken over, caving in without a fight the moment that Matt, in the guise of Sinclair International, had appeared on the financial horizon. Building upon the banking and business foundation left to him by his father John Sinclair, who had died when his son was only ten years of age, Matt had swiftly and relentlessly expanded his empire. His progress to fame and ever-increasing fortune had been littered with the debris of those who didn't understand his compulsive urge to win—at any cost.

A hard, tough and ruthless man, Matt operated his

business in exactly the same way that he ran his own personal life—with harsh, merciless efficiency. And of course, Francesca told herself with a sigh, she should have realised that *that* was why the disturbing, upsetting dream had returned to haunt her. You didn't need a very high IQ to know that it had been caused by deeply buried anxiety—a subconscious fear of meeting the man who had so blighted her young life.

Giving another heavy sigh, Francesca turned back into the room. Knowing the root cause of her problem was one thing—having to deal with it was, unfortunately, quite another. Removing a pair of white cotton trousers and an aquamarine sleeveless T-shirt from her open suitcase, she tried to force some courage into her shrinking veins.

She wasn't asking for anything that was likely to cause Matt any trouble—rather the reverse, in fact. She was merely hoping to persuade him to add his signature to a legal document—thereby breaking the trust set up on her father's death, and enabling her to get hold of the large amount of money she was not due to inherit until she was thirty.

Thirty! she thought incredulously. She would probably be a wizened old hag by then! Why should she have to wait six more years for something that was rightfully hers? And surely Matt would be glad to be rid of an annoying burden which he'd clearly never wanted in the first place?

Over the past three years, Francesca had signally failed to find the answer to the question why her father, that shrewd and successful industrialist Sir Dennis Patterson, had nominated Matt in his will as the main

trustee of his estate. Although he'd always been scru-
pulously fair to his young stepson, carefully guarding
and supervising the boy's financial inheritance from his
own father, as Matt grew up it had become abundantly
clear that the two men didn't like one another.

Not that she could entirely blame Matt for his
jaundiced view of her father, nor for his scathing
remarks about Sir Dennis's totally selfish way of life.
Her father had always done exactly as he'd pleased—
with everyone else coming a poor second, even his
much-loved second wife Elizabeth.

Lifting a brush and trying to tame her cloud of
tangled long blonde hair, Francesca's blue eyes grew
cloudy and sorrowful for a moment as she recalled the
warmth and affectionate care of the only mother she'd
ever known.

Elizabeth Sinclair had been a widow of thirty-two
with a young son, Matthew, aged ten, when she'd
decided to pay a visit to her old family home in
England—not having set foot in the country since her
marriage to an American banker, John Sinclair. It was
a fortunate day for Francesca when Elizabeth, after a
whirlwind courtship, married Sir Dennis. His new bride
had immediately insisted on providing a tender, loving
home for the unwanted child of his previous marriage,
and shielding the small girl from the harsh slurs and
savage newspaper headlines about her real mother's
many amorous exploits.

Her stepmother's death, when Francesca was only
just sixteen, had left the girl devastated with grief—the
tragedy made far worse by that disastrous, sordid

confrontation with Matt, from which she had thought she would never recover.

But, of course, she *had*, Francesca now reminded herself firmly. Over the last eight years she'd come to see that everyone had something in their past of which they were deeply ashamed. She'd managed to put the whole squalid episode behind her a long time ago. There was nothing Matt could do to hurt her now. In fact, all she wanted from him was his signature on a legal document—and after she'd obtained that she would never need to see her stepbrother again.

After paying off the taxi which had transported her from the hotel, Francesca looked around her with interest. It was her first visit to the spice island of Grenada, and she'd had no idea of what to expect when she'd been told to arrive at an unknown place called 'Prickly Bay'.

Behind her, the hills were ablaze with hundreds of trees bearing bright orange flowers—immortelle trees, the taxi-driver had called them—while the bay itself appeared to be a wide semicircle of sand, fringed by a tapestry of attractive houses and gardens, interspersed with clumps of palm trees.

Walking down the path which led to a small marina, whose fresh green lawns were dotted with palm and almond trees, Francesca almost gasped aloud at the vista before her. She'd never seen *so* many boats! Every shape and size, from what looked like small dinghys to tall, three-masted elegant yachts, were bobbing peacefully on the blue waters of the sheltered bay. And then, as she sat down on a bench beneath a

tall palm tree, grateful for the shade from the sun
scorching down from above, she suddenly realised that
she had a real problem on her hands.

How on earth was she supposed to know which was
Matt's boat?

If she'd thought about it at all, back in England,
she'd vaguely imagined arriving at a deserted bay with
only a solitary yacht waiting to meet her. But she could
now see that, even if she managed to hire someone
with a small craft to help her to inspect each and every
vessel in the bay, it was likely to take her many hours.
It would, she thought with dismay, be like looking for
a needle in a haystack.

'Is you Miz Patterson?' a voice demanded, and she
looked up quickly to find a huge dark man grinning
down at her.

'Er—yes,' Francesca murmured as the man gave her
another wide friendly smile.

'OK. The boss is waiting for you, so let's hit it!' he
said cheerfully, gesturing towards a small boat tied to a
nearby jetty.

Francesca was well aware that she was a complete
novice—anything she knew about boats could easily be
written on the back of a postage stamp. All the
same. . . 'Are you sure this is quite safe?' she murmured, apprehensively eyeing the small grey inflated
rubber dinghy with a large outboard motor fixed to the
rear.

But the man merely gave a guffaw of jovial laughter.
'No problem! I ain't punctured one in years,' he
assured her, taking her arm and handing her down into
the frail contraption.

Despite her initial misgivings, Francesca was surprised and impressed by the performance of the deli-
cate-looking craft as it zipped over the water. The
man—who announced that his name was Calvin—was
clearly handling the small dinghy with considerable
skill as he manoeuvred his way between the mass of
boats, before speeding towards two vessels anchored at
the mouth of the bay.

As they drew nearer, she could see that one boat
was far larger than the other. Trust Matt to have the
biggest and the best, she thought grimly, staring over
at the name *Wall Street II* painted in large letters on
the stern of a vessel as large, if not larger, than any she
had seen in the South of France. And why his assistant
had said that her stepbrother was 'sailing' in the
Caribbean she had no idea. Surely 'driving' would be
more appropriate? Because this huge boat didn't have
a mast in sight, and was clearly only powered by
goodness knew how many diesel engines.

While Calvin hitched the rubber dinghy to a wide
diving-platform at the rear of the yacht, she looked
over her shoulder at the other vessel lying across the
water. The long sleek lines of the graceful two-masted
schooner were far more her idea of what a yacht should
look like, she decided before turning back and preparing to follow Calvin up a ladder on to the main
deck.

As she followed in the wake of a white-uniformed
member of the crew along a wide, seemingly endless
passageway, it was almost as though her entire res-
piratory system was breaking down, Francesca thought
wildly. She was finding it practically impossible to

control her breathing. Every step she took appeared to be accelerating her inner panic and nervous tension at the forthcoming confrontation.

You've got to keep calm! she cautioned herself. After all, it wasn't as if she was asking for the moon. Once Matt had agreed to break the trust, she could then go ahead with the purchase of the Bond Street art gallery where she worked—now suddenly for sale on the retirement of her boss, Oscar Thornton.

She'd fought against the idea of going cap in hand to Matt, of course. However, there was no other way she could lay her hands on the considerable amount of money needed to purchase the business. And, however much she hated having to confront a man whom she'd vowed never to have anything to do with for the rest of her life, it was now far too late to back out. All her instincts were screaming for her to escape while she could, and it was only a determined resolve not to allow herself to be bullied by Matt which helped her to place one foot in front of the other.

And then suddenly, with a brief knock and the announcement, 'Miss Patterson to see you, sir,' she found herself moving like an automaton as she entered a large room, hardly aware of the almost silent click of the heavy maple door as it closed behind her.

It was some moments before her eyes, still dazzled from the sun's glare, adjusted to the subdued light caused by the smoked-glass windows, which ran floor-to-ceiling around three sides of the enormous space. Then, like a magnet, her gaze was irresistibly drawn to the tall figure sitting behind a huge executive desk at the far end of the room.

Her dream last night had been extraordinarily accurate, she realised with a sinking heart. Because Matthew Sinclair didn't seem to have changed at all over the past years. In fact, if anything, his hard, tanned and handsome features appeared to be more stern and uncompromising than ever. His photographs in the Press had never done him justice, Francesca conceded reluctantly. No celluloid print had ever been able to capture the tough physical aura the man projected, nor reproduce the dynamic sense of power and sheer animal vitality—almost tangible, despite the considerable length of beige carpeting which lay between them.

'Francesca. . .?' he murmured, raising his head to view the slender figure standing across the room.

As she stood there, slim and of average height, with long silvery ash-blonde hair, it was obvious to Matt that his young stepsister had matured into a beautiful woman. Fine bone-structure, and a high forehead over hauntingly vivid aquamarine-blue eyes, wide-spaced and fringed by thick dark lashes, gave the girl a faintly medieval appearance; the sort of looks which would have recommended her to artists such as Michelangelo and Leonardo da Vinci.

'You've actually managed to arrive on time, I see,' Matt said drily.

Her cheeks flushing as she registered the cool, ironic tone in his deep voice—and the reminder that punctuality had never been her strong point—Francesca nervously cleared her throat.

'Hello, Matt,' she muttered, desperately trying to pull herself together and ignore those broad, muscular shoulders beneath the short-sleeved black silk shirt—a colour which seemed to emphasise his deeply tanned skin. 'It—er—it's nice to see you again.'

He didn't reply, merely greeting her banal remark with a slight, sardonic nod of his dark head. There was obviously very little that escaped those piercing green eyes, like hard chips of emerald ice, which were now subjecting her to a deliberately slow insulting appraisal. And, even as her hackles rose in self-defence, Francesca could feel a cold shiver of fear quivering down her spine.

'I was told you wanted to see me,' he said at last, his powerful body shifting slightly as he impatiently waved her towards a chair in front of the desk. 'I imagine that it must be an urgent matter,' he added with silky menace. 'Because I can see no other reason for you to disturb my vacation.'

It wasn't difficult to remember why she hated this man, Francesca told herself grimly as she forced her unwilling legs to walk across the carpet.

'I've already told your personal assistant in New York exactly why I needed to meet you,' she reminded him tersely as she sank down on to the hard chair. 'I really can't see the point——'

'I never make a decision without hearing the full facts for myself,' he drawled. 'So, why don't you tell me all about your problem?' he added, leaning forward to push a button on his desk.

He must think she was a complete idiot! Francesca's normally full lips tightened, anger rapidly taking over from her initial fear and trepidation. Did he imagine that she'd forgotten one of his basic business practices? Because, if so, he was very much mistaken!

'Well?' He drummed his fingers impatiently on the desk.

'I'm not telling you a damn thing—not while you've got that hidden tape-recorder going!' she snapped. 'What I have to say is private—and it's going to remain that way,' she added defiantly.

His mouth twisted into a grim smile. 'Well, well, well. . .it would seem that my little sister has grown up at last,' he drawled with sardonic amusement as he leaned forward to cancel the recording.

'I'm *not* your little sister,' she snapped. She could feel her temper about to erupt any minute, and her cheeks became flushed with the effort to control it. 'The only thing we have in common is that your mother married my father. There is no blood relationship between us—thank goodness!' she added with feeling.

'You have just echoed my own sentiments exactly,' he agreed with a silky detachment which she found absolutely maddening. Her blue eyes flashed with suppressed fury as she watched him rise and, with his customary lithe movement, walk over to a coffee machine set on a table across the room.

'I dislike being disturbed when I'm working,' he explained. 'Would you care to join me in a cup of coffee?'

I'd rather throw it in your face, she thought rebelliously, but contented herself with giving him a curt nod.

How *could* she ever have imagined that she'd been

madly in love with Matt? An extremely foolish sixteen-year-old at the time, Francesca knew that she had been the victim of a silly teenage crush which had unfortunately grown out of control.

A small private boarding-school, set deep in the English countryside, was hardly the ideal place to obtain an adequate knowledge of sexual matters. In fact, sex had played no part in her adoration of the man in front of her. It had been a typical case of chaste, innocent puppy-love—far more akin to fairy-tales than the real world. She very much suspected that if he had asked her to lie down and die for him she would have certainly done her best to do so! And, if it all hadn't ended so disastrously, she might have been able to look back and laugh at the young girl who had clearly been as green as grass, completely unable to cope with the powerful attraction she'd felt towards a man—who was also her stepbrother—and almost ten years older than herself.

A movement at the edge of her peripheral vision interrupted her thoughts, Francesca's pale cheeks flushing as the original object of her adoration placed a cup and saucer on the desk in front of her.

'All right, Francesca. We've renewed our—er—family acquaintance. So I think it's about time you got around to telling me why you're here, don't you?' he said drily, moving back to resume his seat. 'I understand that you want my agreement to the termination of your father's trust. Am I correct?'

'Yes.' She nodded, and then took a deep breath before continuing. 'As you probably know, since leaving the Courtauld Institute I've been working at Quenell and Thornton's Art Gallery in Bond Street.'

She paused for a moment, but when he merely continued to regard her silently she went on to explain that the owner of the gallery, Oscar Thornton, was due to retire. Without any family or close relatives interested in taking over from him, he'd agreed to sell her the business.

'I'm not intending to run it all by myself,' she assured Matt earnestly. 'It will be a joint venture with another assistant, Rupert ffinch-Rawlings, with whom I've been working for the past two years.' She gave a slight laugh. 'Since Rupert's related to at least half of the landed gentry in *Debrett*, his connections are likely to prove very useful!'

'But I take it that he has no money to put into the business. . .?' Matt queried shrewdly.

'Er—no, I'm afraid that he hasn't,' she admitted. 'And that's the whole point, you see? In order to buy the business from Oscar I'm going to need a large amount of capital—although it's only about half the sum that my father left in trust for me.'

'And you are asking me to help you break the trust?'

'Exactly!' She gave Matt a tentative smile, almost sagging with relief. She would never have believed that her dreaded stepbrother could be so reasonable. Maybe she'd been guilty of misjudging him all these years? 'I'm sure you'll be glad to get rid of something that's been nothing but a nuisance,' she continued with a slight shrug of her shoulders. 'In fact, I've never understood why Dad chose you, of all people, as one of my trustees. And as for making me wait until I'm thirty before I get the money—well, it's simply too ridiculous for words!'

'Hmm. . .' Matt murmured non-committally, before enquiring, 'What about the other trustee? How does your father's lawyer feel about this—er—scheme of yours?'

Francesca had always known that this was going to be the sticky point. Unfortunately, with those hard emerald eyes boring into her skull, it was almost impossible for her to try and bluff her way out of a tough corner.

'He's left the decision up to you,' she muttered lamely. In fact, Sir Dennis Patterson's lawyer had expressed himself quite forcefully on the subject. He'd been extremely reluctant to even consider the idea—not until she had obtained Matthew Sinclair's whole-hearted agreement, and his signature on a legally drawn-up agreement.

There was a long silence between them, before Matt shrugged his shoulders and leaned idly back in his chair.

'I can't see any reason why I should agree to your request,' he announced in a bored tone of voice.

'But. . .but I need your help!' she cried, unable to believe that he was really turning her down.

'Help. . .?' he drawled mockingly. 'Why should I help you? You appear to be earning a reasonable salary, and you also have a considerable private income left to you by your father. I wouldn't have said that you're exactly on the poverty line, Francesca!' he mocked.

Her cheeks flushed. 'I never pretended that I was,' she protested. 'I know that I'm very well off as far as most people are concerned. But that's not the point. I want to buy the shop, and——'

He raised an imperious hand. 'I've already heard what you have to say, and I don't see how I can help you.'

'But I'm not asking you to put a hand in *your* pocket. I only want the opportunity to freely handle my *own* money!' she wailed.

There wasn't so much as a flicker of emotion or compassion visible on his hard, stern features, and the ensuing silence seemed to reverberate around the room as Francesca desperately tried to think of something that might cause him to change his mind.

'Is it the fact that I want to buy an art gallery? Maybe you don't like modern art, and——'

'On the contrary,' he drawled, his lips twisting into a slight, humourless smile. 'I have a substantial holding in Southeby Parke-Bennett in New York, and I also own a gallery, in Los Angeles, specialising in twentieth-century paintings.'

'So why can't you release the trust?' she demanded, close to tears with frustration.

Matt shrugged his broad shoulders. 'I didn't say I *couldn't* do as you wish. I merely don't see why I *should*.'

'Well, thank you—for absolutely *nothing*!' she ground out furiously, leaping to her feet and glaring angrily down at him. 'I might have know that the great Matthew Sinclair would be far too busy—counting his millions of dollars, no doubt!—to bother himself with his sister's problems.'

'I thought we'd just agreed that you weren't my

sister,' he drawled coolly, a note of steely warning in his voice which she refused to heed.

'If I hadn't been so fond of your mother I'd say that you were a complete bastard!' she retorted bitterly, throwing caution to the winds as she trembled with rage and fury. 'You've always hated me, haven't you? I might have known that it was a mad idea to come here—totally *insane* to imagine that you'd raise one finger to help me.'

'That's quite enough!'

'You are so right!' she hissed through clenched teeth, spinning on her heels and walking swiftly towards the door.

'Not so fast!' Somehow he'd reached the door before her, his muscular figure a towering, formidable wall preventing her escape as he gripped hold of her arm.

'Let go of me!' she snapped, glaring up at the harsh, indomitable expression on Matt's face, bitterly aware of her erratic heartbeat at his close proximity. The air between them seemed charged with electrical force, her body quivering with fear at the knowledge that he still possessed the power to disturb her.

'Certainly—when you've calmed down,' he replied smoothly, propelling her reluctant figure back across the room.

'You. . .you can't keep me here!' she protested, inwardly cursing the husky, breathless note in her voice as he pushed her down into a chair.

Matt gave a harsh bark of laughter. 'Oh, yes, I can. Or were you intending to swim back to the shore, hmm. . .?'

Leaning against the edge of the desk, he allowed her

a few moments to realise that she was well and truly
stuck, before adding, 'While I have severe reservations
about your proposed venture into the art world—a far
more risky business than you seem to realise—I might
be persuaded to change my mind.

'Oh, yes. . .?' She gazed up at him suspiciously, not
daring to trust the faint glimmer of hope flickering
through her veins.

'I have a small irritating problem on my hands—and
I think it's one which you can help me to solve,' he
drawled. 'Some important guests are arriving here from
the States tomorrow, and quite unexpectedly I find
myself in need of a chef.'

'A *chef*?' Her blue eyes widened as she stared at him
with amazement. 'Do you mean "chef" as in "kitchen"?'

'Precisely.'

'But I don't understand.' She shook her head in
bewilderment.

His dark brows drew together in an irritated frown.
'I thought you'd spent six months doing a cordon bleu
course before going to university?'

'Well, yes. Dad seemed to think it was a good
idea. . .' Francesca's voice trailed away as she slowly
began to realise the nature of the deal he was
proposing.

'Do you mean. . .? Are you seriously suggesting
that, if I agree to cook for your guests, you will help
me gain control of my money?' When he nodded his
dark head, she gave a gasp of incredulous laughter.
'You must be crazy! I'll bet there are hundreds of local
people who are better qualified for the job than I am.'

'You may be right,' he agreed drily. 'But, unfortunately, none of them are available at the moment.'

She gave a weak laugh. 'Oh, come on, Matt—this whole idea of yours is too ridiculous! Other than the occasional dinner party, it's a long time since I've done any serious cooking.'

'I'm sure you'll manage.' His expression became hard and forceful. 'In fact, my dear Francesca, if you want me to relinquish the trusteeship of your father's estate, I don't see that you have any choice in the matter!'

She stared up at him with loathing. Here was this man who—if he was all *that* desperate—could well afford to fly a professional chef over from New York to cater for his guests. So why on earth was he pressuring her into a job for which he must know she was supremely unqualified?

Waves of resentment and tiredness swept over her weary body. It had been a long flight yesterday, and she was still feeling the effects of jet lag. Goodness knows what sort of game Matt thought he was playing, but she'd got the message loud and clear: unless she agreed to his mad proposal, she hadn't a hope of buying the art gallery. Unfortunately it very much looked as if that hateful man, Matthew Sinclair, had her well and truly over a barrel!

CHAPTER TWO

FRANCESCA couldn't ever remember a time when she'd felt quite so tired and exhausted. Wiping the perspiration from her brow, she sank wearily down on to a settee, closing her eyes as she leaned back on the soft cushions and savoured the late-afternoon breeze wafting in through the open hatch above.

She was no longer wondering why Matt had press-ganged her into acting as a chef—although, as it had turned out, 'chief cook and bottle-washer' would have been a far more accurate title. She now knew that, as far as Matt was concerned, her arrival on his boat this morning must have seemed like manna from heaven. Maybe, if she *had* realised the full extent of the problems facing him, she might not have caved in quite so easily to the pressure he was exerting. Unfortunately it was too late to do anything about it now, she thought gloomily, grimacing with annoyance at herself for being such a push-over.

However, six hours ago, as she'd sat in his enormous office, she—poor fool!—had been far too occupied with her own problems to do more than wonder why that hard, shrewd businessman should be making such an extraordinary bargain. And all because he needed a cook! It seemed to be a very trivial reason—especially when she would be getting so much for very little effort.

'I still think you're mad,' she'd told him bluntly. 'But I'm not in a position to look a gift-horse in the mouth.'

'No, you're not,' he'd agreed drily. 'So—we have a deal, hmm. . .?'

Francesca gave a bemused shake of her blonde head. 'Well, yes, I suppose we have. But. . .but I'm not moving from this chair until I have it in writing,' she added trenchantly.

The air between them crackled ominously for a moment, sparks of anger glinting in Matt's icy green eyes.

'Are you implying that you don't trust me?' he demanded coldly.

'Yes!'

There was a long, tense silence which seemed to last forever, before he gave a snort of wry amusement. Francesca, who had been unconsciously holding her breath in fear and trepidation, sighed in relief as he calmly opened a drawer and withdrew some headed notepaper.

'You're quite right—never trust anyone,' he murmured, his pen flowing quickly over two pieces of white paper. 'And especially not someone who appears to be offering you a bargain,' he added with a grim smile as he placed the letters on the desk.

'I think that's a perfectly disgusting philosophy,' she retorted, leaning forward and quickly scanning what he had written. 'Hey—what's this about my acting as a cook, "for two weeks"?' She glared at him. 'I can't possibly be away from work that long.'

Matt shrugged his broad shoulders. 'That's the deal—take it or leave it.'

'Oh—all right,' she sighed, knowing that she hadn't really any choice in the matter.

Taking the pen he handed her, she quickly countersigned both pieces of paper, consoling herself with the thought that Oscar Thornton was bound to be reasonable about the delay in her return to work. Especially when he learned that she was now going to be able to buy his art gallery. 'I must let Oscar know the good news,' she told Matt.

'International phone calls from Grenada can be difficult,' he said. 'However, I can get one of my secretaries to fax through the "good news", if you like.'

She didn't care for the dry, sardonic note in his voice. However, since it was obviously going to expedite matters, she nodded her head in agreement. Maybe things weren't going to be so bad, after all, Francesca told herself, making a determined effort to look on the bright side of the situation. All she had to do was to try and stagger through the next two weeks. And, while it clearly wasn't going to be a bed of roses, this huge motor-yacht was bound to have a glamorous kitchen to work in. She'd *die* rather than admit it to Matt, of course. But, although she was obviously out of practice, it might be quite fun to do some creative cooking.

'Well, I don't know what you have in mind—food-wise,' she told him as he put his copy of their agreement away in a drawer. 'However, I suppose the first thing I ought to do is to inspect your kitchen.'

'On board ship, it's called a galley,' he corrected her.

'Kitchen—galley—whatever. . .' She waved a dismissive hand. 'I'm assuming that this huge floating gin-palace of yours has most of the basic foodstuffs, and plenty of cooking utensils?'

Matt, whose lips had tightened at her caustic reference to the size and splendour of his yacht, stared at her silently for a moment.

'Oh, yes, indeed it has,' he agreed in a slow drawl.

'In that case, I'd better have a look around it.'

'Ah. . .no, that won't be necessary.'

She shrugged her shoulders. 'Well, it's up to you, of course. But don't blame me if I can't produce a dish simply because I haven't got the right herbs or spices.' She tucked her own copy of their bargain into her shoulder-bag, and rose to her feet. 'And now I really must get back to my hotel.'

'No.'

'What do you mean?'

Since she knew that Matt had never gone back on a deal, the painful knot of nerves in her stomach had begun to subside. But now, as she frowned across the desk at him, Francesca could feel the anxiety and tension rising within her once more.

'I'm afraid that you seem to be labouring under a misapprehension,' he drawled. 'I don't require your services on *this* boat, for which I have a perfectly adequate chef. As far as I'm concerned, my dear Francesca,' he added, his lips twitching in silent humour, 'you have just been engaged as a cook for my schooner, *Silver Lady*.'

'Your *what*?'

Matt pushed a switch on the side of the desk, and,

following his gaze, she turned to see the smoked-glass windows at the end of the room, slowly gliding open.

Almost in a dream, Francesca found herself drifting over the carpet and out on to the deck, squinting in the bright sunlight as she stared at the yacht riding at anchor across the bay.

'But I can't! I mean, I. . .' She turned to find Matt standing beside her. 'You must be out of your mind! I don't know the first thing about sailing. In fact—until today—I don't think I've ever been in anything larger than a rowing-boat.'

'You're not being asked to *sail* the yacht,' he drawled mockingly. 'I merely require you to provide first-class meals for my guests.'

'*Merely*. . .?' she echoed bitterly, glowering up at him before turning to look back at the schooner. 'I bet there isn't room to swing a cat in that yacht's kitchen.'

'Galley!'

'You know what I mean!' she snapped angrily. 'And anyway, if you've already got a chef—why on earth do you need me?'

'Pierre is very gifted but, alas, very—er—very temperamental.' Matt shrugged his broad shoulders. 'And, since I value his services, I've agreed to allow him to remain here, on this yacht.'

'It sounds as though Pierre is no fool!' she retorted caustically. 'I'm sorry, Matt. I might have managed all right on this Cunard-type boat of yours. But a jolly, yo-ho-ho life on the ocean wave is simply *not* my scene.'

His eyes glinted with amusement for a moment. 'One should always welcome a new experience.'

'Thank you—but I'll pass on this one!' she snapped. 'Trying to cook in a force-nine gale—or whatever—is an experience I can well do without!'

'I have no doubt that you'll manage,' he replied evenly.

'Oh—for heaven's sake!' she exclaimed impatiently. 'Haven't you been listening to a word I've been saying?'

'I fear it is *you* who haven't been listening to me,' he informed her bluntly. 'As far as I'm concerned, you have just agreed to serve as my chef for two weeks.'

'But I didn't agree to cook on *that* boat!' She gestured wildly in the direction of the schooner.

'Too bad.'

As he gave a bored, offhand shrug of his shoulders, she almost choked with fury. The double-dealing swine! He'd quite deliberately led her up the garden path, letting her assume that she'd be working in the comfortable luxury of this mini-liner. Instead of which she now faced what she suspected were hot, cramped conditions in a boat that looked *extremely* dangerous.

'I. . . I won't do it!' she declared vehemently, turning to go back into the room.

She had hardly taken more than a step before his hand grasped her arm, swinging her around to face him with such force that she found herself clasped to his firm chest. Shocked by the abruptness of his action, she shivered nervously as she gazed up into his hard green eyes.

'I've had quite enough of this nonsense.' His lips tightened ominously. 'I need a cook. You want to be able to handle your own money. As far as I'm concerned, we've made a deal. And I have your signed agreement to that effect—remember?'

'You don't understand. . .' she gasped. 'That other yacht of yours looks terrifying. I could drown, or——'

'Nonsense! In fact, it's a far safer vessel than the one we're on now.'

'But. . .but I'm sure to be seasick,' she wailed.

'If you are, you'll get over it,' he retorted brutally. 'And don't bother trying to complain about there being no nightlife, because you'll just have to do without it for two weeks!'

Despite the hot sun beating down from above, a chill shivered down her spine. The sudden silence and tension between them was almost claustrophobic, and she was bitterly aware of the hot colour flooding her cheeks.

She had hoped and prayed that he might have forgotten their last traumatic confrontation in the South of France all those years ago. But now, with his cold green eyes glinting down into hers, she knew— *with absolute certainty*—that the agonising, shameful scene was still just as fresh in his memory as it was in her own.

It was then that she finally realised just what an insane idiot she'd been. She should *never* have come within a million miles of Matthew Sinclair!

'Please let me go,' she begged as his fingers bit into her arm.

'No.'

She trembled at the harsh note of determination in his voice. 'But I—er—I must go back to the hotel. I have to collect my suitcase, and. . .and settle the bill,' she told him breathlessly, trying to wriggle away from his tall, dominating figure.

'You're not going anywhere!' Matt gave a harsh sardonic laugh as he gazed down at her flushed cheeks and the wide blue eyes, whose long lashes fluttered nervously beneath his steady gaze. 'We've struck a bargain, Francesca—and I intend to see that you keep it!'

Pressed so tightly against his body, she felt her legs begin to tremble as she became aware of the warmth of his skin through the thin black silk shirt, open at the neck to display the strong column of his tanned throat. His proximity was playing havoc with her senses, her eyes drawn inexorably to his formidable jawline and the cruel sensuality of his lips.

'You deliberately tricked me!' she gasped, striving to tear herself away from his dominating figure.

'Ah. . .but surely I told you to beware of gaining too easy a bargain?' he enquired with hard irony, his muscular arm easily restraining her violently struggling figure. 'However, you were just a little too eager, Francesca, weren't you? Too anxious to get your hands on a large sum of money. In fact,' he added cruelly, 'you're turning out to be an avaricious, greedy little bitch—just like your own mother Natalie!'

Pushed beyond the limits of endurance, Francesca brought up her free hand and slapped his face as hard as she could. She'd been itching to do so ever since discovering how Matt had double-crossed her, and in the end the temptation was just *too* much for her to resist. For a brief moment afterwards she felt an overwhelming sense of satisfaction. But when he didn't move, merely staring down at her in silence—the red imprint of her hand clearly visible on his tanned skin—she felt ready to sink through the highly polished deck of his yacht in an agony of shame and remorse.

'I'm sorry, I. . .'

'That was very silly of you,' he hissed softly, the dangerous underlying threat in his voice causing her to feel almost sick with fear.

'I didn't mean. . .' she gabbled nervously. 'I know I shouldn't have. . .' But it was far too late. As she stared up into his eyes, like a rabbit hypnotised by a car's headlamps, there seemed nothing she could do to prevent his arms closing about her like a steel trap.

When his dark head came down towards her she made one last, weak attempt to break free of his embrace. And then his mouth was on her lips, ruthlessly forcing them to part as he explored the warm inner moistness of her mouth with a brutality which was clearly intended more as a punishment than a pleasure.

She fought him as hard as she could, trying in vain to push him away. But she had no hope of escape. His lips burned and demanded her surrender, the kiss deepening until she was barely able to breathe. And then, just when she was certain that she was going to faint dead away, the remorseless pressure eased, his lips becoming warm and persuasive as they softly coaxed and teased away all resistance. Her pulse was racing out of control, her slim figure shaking with long-suppressed emotions as she sank beneath a tidal wave of desire.

Well out of her depth and drowning in a pool of dark passion, she moaned and shivered uncontrollably as his lips trailed slowly down her throat. It was some moments before her eyelids fluttered open, her pupils dazed by the strong rays of the sun. Slowly, through the blinding brilliance, she saw Matt looking down at her with his mouth twisted in a cruel, sardonic smile.

A second later she was free, as he released her before crossing the deck to stand with his back to her, staring down into the water. Dazed and shattered, her heart still racing out of control, Francesca gazed over at his tall, indomitable figure, quite unable to say or do anything.

It was some moments before Matt turned back to face her. His face was slightly flushed beneath his deep tan, his green eyes glittering like hard emerald chips as he leaned casually against the railing at the edge of the deck. Unlike her, he seemed to have no difficulty in finding his voice.

'Don't *ever* try to slap me again! Because if you do I promise that I'll put you over my knee—and beat the living daylights out of you!'

'You. . .you shouldn't have said that about Natalie,' she whispered huskily, flinching beneath the hard, scornful tone in his voice. 'I know that my mother isn't exactly——'

'We both know that Natalie is a tramp,' he said with cold brutality. 'Not content with trapping your father by getting pregnant—if I remember the facts correctly, you were born only a few weeks after your father put a ring on her finger—she upped and ran away with that Italian prince when you were only two.'

'That still doesn't give you any right to——'

'Since then,' he continued, ignoring her interjection, 'I wouldn't like to try and count the number of husbands and lovers she's had—all featured prominently in the world's Press. If it hadn't been for *my* mother, God knows what would have happened to you. As far as I can see,' he added caustically, 'you don't just look like Natalie—it seems as though you're turning out to behave exactly like her as well.'

'I'm *not* like her!' Francesca cried bitterly. 'You've always made that mistake. And why should you care about her, anyway? Natalie had run away and left Dad and me long before you and your mother came on the scene.'

'My mother's life was blighted by that woman,' Matt told her roughly. 'It got so bad at one time that she dreaded opening the newspapers and having to read— yet again—all the highly colourful, scandalous reports concerning the *ex* Lady Patterson!'

Francesca frowned in puzzlement, pushing a shaking hand through her ash-blonde hair. 'But it wasn't really like that,' she protested. 'I mean. . .of course your mother sometimes got a bit fed up with Natalie's "goings-on", as she used to call it. But most of the time she merely laughed about it, and used to tell me that, if and when I got to know Natalie, I wouldn't find her half as black as she was painted.'

'Don't be such a fool. Can't you see that my mother was just trying to protect you?' Matt told her scornfully.

'But. . .but she was quite right,' Francesca told him. 'Although I didn't meet or get to know Natalie until after I'd left school, she was. . .well, if you want to know the truth, I found her a bit of a disappointment.'

'My God—now I've heard it all!' he ground out in disgust.

'No—you don't understand. I'd expected to meet a scarlet woman, or. . .or some kind of outrageous *femme fatale*, but she wasn't like that at all. In fact, she was quite a funny and amusing, still very attractive woman, who was a lot quieter than I'd imagined.'

Matt gave a harsh bark of laughter. 'She certainly seems to have fooled you!'

'No, I don't think so,' Francesca said firmly, determined to put her mother's case as fairly as possible. 'I'm not saying that she's particularly clever, or intelligent, because she clearly isn't. But Natalie's been happily married for the past ten years to that pop star, Ziggy Malone. And, whenever I stay with her in New York, she always seems to be far more interested in cooking the sort of meals Ziggy likes, and redecorating the apartment, than in any spectacular nightlife. Quite honestly, Matt,' Francesca added earnestly, 'she may be silly—but she's certainly not evil.'

He shrugged his shoulders dismissively. 'As far as I can see, you know *nothing* about your mother.'

'And you do, I suppose,' she retorted sarcastically.

'Oh, yes. . .indeed I do!' His lips widened into a malicious, sardonic grin. 'How long did you say Natalie had been married to her pop star?'

'About ten years, I think.'

'Ah. Well, *eight* years ago—just before I had to leave New York and fly to France because my own mother was dying—I had the dubious pleasure of being propositioned in a nightclub by Natalie!'

'I. . . I don't believe you!' she gasped hoarsely.

'We had a great time—she even invited me back to her apartment,' he said, ignoring Francesca's agonised words of denial. 'And it wasn't until it was almost too late that I discovered *who* she was—and just *what* a mistake I'd nearly made!'

'No!' Francesca moaned, feeling sick as she leaned weakly against a nearby pillar. 'You must be lying. . .'

'Oh, no, I'm not!' He gave a cruel laugh. 'After all, you're quite right: Natalie is, or was, a very attractive woman. And, although I don't wish to appear too immodest, I can assure you that she clearly fancied having me in her bed.'

'You're disgusting!'

He shrugged his broad shoulders. 'Maybe. But it was nothing to the disgust I felt when—within the short space of a few weeks—I discovered that I could have had both of you,' he said brutally. 'Mother *and* daughter—how about that?'

Francesca could only stare blindly back at him, the blood draining from her face, leaving it pale and ashen with shock. It seemed a long time before she could force her dazed mind to comprehend the full significance of what he'd just said.

Matt's ghastly story could have been a complete fabrication, of course. But he'd always been extremely truthful, and there seemed no reason on earth why he should tell such terrible lies. Besides. . . *Oh, Natalie!* she groaned inwardly, knowing in her heart of hearts that her silly, wayward mother would have been quite capable of picking up strange men in night-clubs. But. . .but surely there must be some other rational explanation for the older woman's behaviour?

'I—er—I'm sure that you must be mistaken about this,' Francesca muttered. 'And. . .and if you aren't. . .well, I suppose it's one of those awful coincidences that could happen to anyone. . . I mean. . .'

'I admire your sense of loyalty.' He gave another of his cruel laughs. 'However, I must point out that Natalie was a married woman, while I was at least fourteen years younger than she was. It's not a pretty story, is it?'

'And what about *your* part in this affair?' Francesca lashed back, consumed with hatred for this loathsome man. 'What were *you* doing, trying to pick up a woman who was almost old enough to be your mother? After all. . .' she lifted a trembling hand to her lips '. . .it was *you* who assaulted me just now.'

'That was merely to teach you a lesson,' he snapped tersely. 'And I hope it's one you'll heed. Now—am I going to have any more nonsense from you?' he added, taking a threatening step towards her. 'Or are you going to be sensible, and give me your word that you'll keep to our bargain?'

Any resistance Francesca might have had—after the long flight from London, and the nervous exhaustion of forcing herself to face Matt after all these years— had all long since drained away. She was still feeling devastated by his kiss and the terrible story about Natalie. So, even though she despised herself for being so craven, she simply didn't have the reserves of strength to defy him any further.

'Yes, all right,' she muttered, sighing heavily as she stared blindly down at the polished surface of the deck. 'I. . . I promise that I'll honour our deal.'

'All the same—I think I'll have your passport, if you don't mind,' he said, putting out his hand. 'I don't want you to be tempted to try an escape back to London the first moment I turn my back.'

'I've already said that I'll keep to your rotten bargain,' she ground out through gritted teeth, reaching into her bag and reluctantly handing him her passport. 'What more do you want—blood?'

'No, this will do nicely!' he murmured, in parody of the advertisement.

If she'd had the energy she would have cheerfully killed him as his dry, sardonic laughter had echoed around the deck. Even now, six hours after that confrontation, as she sat here in the saloon of the schooner, *Silver Lady*, Francesca was still simmering with anger.

It wasn't just the fact that she hadn't been able to return to her hotel that bugged her—although she hated the idea of someone else packing up her clothes. What had *really* put the lid on a disastrous day, and about which she was still simmering with rage, had been the discovery that Matt had somehow managed to double-cross her yet again!

When Calvin had brought her across to the graceful schooner she'd been so relieved to get away from Matt that she hadn't given a thought to what she'd find once she got on board. And who could blame her? Especially when the exterior paintwork, sails and decking had all looked so immaculate. However, as soon as she'd descended the companion-way down into the main living-quarters, Francesca had quickly discovered her mistake.

It was utterly filthy! Looking with dazed eyes around the large saloon, filled with what seemed to be a mountain of beer cans, empty rum bottles and various bags of rubbish, she'd gingerly picked her way forward towards the cabins. They, too, looked as if they'd been recently occupied by a rugby scrum: sheets and pillow-cases thrown all over the place, and damp towels hanging over every door.

Returning to the saloon, Francesca had called out to Calvin, who'd been tinkering with some machinery at the rear of the yacht.

'What on earth has been going on here?' she demanded when he popped his head through a hatch. 'I've never seen such a mess. No wonder Pierre—or whatever his name is—refused to set foot on this boat. I can't even bear to look in the—er—galley, for fear of what I might find!'

'Yeah, the boss was as mad as a hornet!' Calvin said with a smile before explaining that Matt had lent the schooner to some male business friends. Apparently, instead of soberly working through the long weekend on a proposed business take-over, they had fallen willing victims to the dire effects of Grenadian rum.

'I guess those guys have got *real* sore heads!' Calvin laughed. 'I do know they was all looking kinda pale and shaking when they left yesterday. Still, the boss says as how you'll soon have the mess all cleared up.'

'Oh—he does, does he?' she hissed furiously. 'Well, you can just tell your "boss" that if, and when, he next sets foot on this boat, *he'd better be wearing a bullet-proof vest!*'

For some reason, Calvin seemed to think that was very funny, but Francesca had completely lost her sense of humour. However, even she could see that she wasn't going to get anywhere by refusing to clean up the yacht—a job which had taken many hours of hard physical labour. However, as she now sat utterly exhausted on one of the settees in the main saloon, she did at least have the satisfaction of knowing that the beautiful boat had been returned to its rightful state.

While she had been working, Calvin had gone to fetch her suitcase from the hotel, returning with a mass of boxes full of provisions, and the news that Matt was intending to join her for dinner tonight.

The damned cheek of the man! He must know what a traumatic and gruelling day it had been for her. He really wanted his pound of flesh, didn't he? Grinding her teeth with rage, Francesca knew that she hadn't a hope of providing anything other than cold meat and salad. She didn't even know how to work that odd-looking stove in the galley, for heaven's sake! While it appeared to be supported by some contrivance which kept it level and steady despite the gentle movement of the boat, she could see that it would be some time before she felt confident enough to use it. So, if Matt thought that he would be getting *haute cuisine* tonight—he was sadly mistaken!

Sending back the message that if he *did* have the nerve to expect a meal, he was likely to be given strychnine soufflé, followed by prawns in prussic acid had done little more than to release some of her furious pent-up anger. She still felt as if she could sleep for a week. Maybe a shower would do something to revive her weary body.

Wiping the dripping perspiration from her brow— goodness, it was hot!—Francesca eased her tired muscles off the settee and made her way to the rear of the boat. As she passed through the galley she couldn't help taking a pride in its fresh appearance. She'd been deeply depressed at her first sight of her domain for the next two weeks. But, now that all the mess had been cleared away, and the stainless-steel surface of the long work-top had been polished, she was feeling a whole lot better.

It had been a relief to discover that the cooking area was larger than she'd first thought, the equipment including a microwave, as well as a refrigerator and deep-freeze cabinet—almost essential items in this sweltering hot climate. On top of which Francesca had been amazed to find the galley also contained a small washing-machine and tumble-drier. And, now that she'd stowed away most of the stores Calvin had brought on board, she felt slightly more optimistic about her ability to cope with the job that Matt had so cruelly forced on her. There was still a large wicker hamper on the floor, but she decided to leave the investigation of its contents until after she'd had a shower.

Groaning with pleasure beneath the cold, fine needle-spray of the remarkably efficient shower, Francesca tried to comfort herself with the realistic, sensible thought that she only had to endure two weeks on this yacht. Even if it turned out to be fourteen days of sheer purgatory—and she very much feared that it would—she'd have gained her main objective. She would be free, at last, to do what she wanted with her own money. *And* she'd never have to see Matt again. How about *that* for a real bonus?

Towelling herself dry, and deliberately trying not to think of the bewildering emotions engendered by Matt's kiss earlier in the day, she walked slowly into her bedroom. Calvin had told her that 'the boss' had left instructions for her to choose one of two large cabins at the rear of the boat. She'd been surprised to find how cleverly the double beds had been fitted into the design, and just how much hanging and storage space had been provided.

Francesca knew that she ought to unpack her case. But the soft mattress and fresh clean sheets looked so inviting that she couldn't resist the temptation to lie down for a moment. In fact, she thought sleepily, she'd got plenty of time to deal with the rest of the jobs which needed doing. It wouldn't matter if she put her feet up—just for five minutes. . .

It was a loud thump on the stern of the yacht that eventually woke her. Confused, and still half asleep, she grabbed a towel to cover her naked body before hurriedly leaving her cabin. Just about to climb the steps leading up on to the rear deck, she paused for a moment. Although she was still feeling dazed and disorientated, she realised that she didn't know who was boarding the vessel—those footsteps, now walking across the deck above, could belong to anyone! A vision of the large wooden rolling-pin in one of the drawers flashed into her mind, and she hurried into the galley.

A moment later she gave a loud scream of terror, taking to her heels and dashing back to the safety of her cabin—only to run slap-bang straight into the arms of the man racing down the small passageway towards her.

'Francesca! What's happened?' Matt demanded urgently as she clung desperately to his tall frame, shrieking with horror.

'*M-Monsters!*' she cried, still clinging to him like a leech. 'There's some. . .some great, *huge* b-black monsters, all over the floor!' She glanced fearfully back over her shoulder, her teeth chattering in fright.

'Calm down! I'm sure there's nothing to be worried about,' he told her firmly. 'Just stay there, and I'll investigate the problem.'

'Don't leave me!' she screeched in panic.

'My dear, Francesca—I thought I was public enemy number one! You've changed your tune rather quickly, haven't you?' he drawled mockingly, before scooping her lightly up in his arms and striding quickly towards the galley.

CHAPTER THREE

'WELL —how was I supposed to know that Calvin had brought some lobsters aboard?' Francesca grumbled, her cheeks flushed with embarrassment.

'"Monsters"!' Matt's shoulders shook with amusement.

'It's all very well for you to laugh,' she muttered, certain that she'd never felt so humiliated in all her life. 'I've never seen any real, *live* ones before. How was I to know that they only go red when they've been cooked?' she added with indignation, tucking her bare feet beneath her on the settee, and tightening the towel firmly about her body.

'I thought you said that you'd done a cordon bleu cookery course?' he drawled.

'So I did. But it didn't include boiling live lobsters,' she said with a shudder. 'And if you think I can face cooking them for supper—you've got another think coming!'

It was some minutes since, screeching with fright, she'd sought the sanctuary of Matt's arms. And when, clinging on to him for dear life, she'd been carried into the galley, she had been mortified to see that the cause of her fear and trembling was merely four large lobsters, which had escaped from their wicker basket.

Stepping over the creatures—and carefully avoiding the large dangerous claws they'd been waving in the

45

air—Matt had deposited her on a settee in the saloon before going back to deal with the problem.

'Anyway, you'll be glad to know that they are all safely back in captivity,' he said, coming over to sit down beside her. 'In fact, while you may have had a shock, they were obviously just as frightened to find themselves in such strange surroundings.'

'Poor things!' She shuddered again. 'As far as I'm concerned, lobster is *definitely* off the menu tonight.'

'Hmm. . .well, it's clear that you can't face any seafood. I'd already got the message, from Calvin, that you were feeling in a rather poisonous frame of mind, so. . .'

'Ha ha!' she ground out.

'. . .you'll be pleased to hear that I asked Pierre to prepare a meal for us.'

Francesca glared at him. 'Quite frankly, it's the least he can do. Not that I blame him for refusing to cook on this boat. If I'd known that it included cleaning up after your business friends I wouldn't have touched it with a barge-pole either!' she added bitterly.

'Well, I must say that you do seem to have done a splendid job,' he said, leaning back and gazing with satisfaction around the large saloon. The maple panelling covering the walls was shining with polish; the glasses, fixed over the bar in a far corner, were shining crystal-clear in the late-afternoon sun, and there wasn't a speck of dust on the deep pile of the rust-coloured carpet.

'Thanks!' she snapped, throwing a glance of thinly veiled venom at the tall muscular figure lounging against the cushions. It was all right for *him*! He hadn't spent most of today on his hands and knees, in this sweltering heat, trying to clean up what had virtually been a pigsty.

In fact, it didn't look as if Matt had done anything more in the hours since she'd last seen him other than have a leisurely shower and change his clothes. He ought to have appeared a mess in that casual pair of lightweight faded denim trousers, topped by an equally casual short-sleeved pale blue shirt. But, unfortunately, there was clearly *no* justice in this life—because Matt was looking even more sensationally attractive than ever.

Resentment welled up inside her, sharpening her tongue. 'I can't think why—when you're so *stinking* rich—you couldn't have organised a team of local cleaners to sort out the mess on this boat.'

'No time,' he replied succinctly. 'My guests are due to arrive here, from the States, early tomorrow morning. So I had to get the yacht cleaned up today.'

'I must have seemed the answer to your prayers,' she muttered sourly. 'Otherwise you might have been forced to get some of those elegant New York girl-friends of yours to roll up their sleeves and do a hard day's work for a change!'

'As opposed to a hard day's night?' he drawled mockingly, his eyes gleaming with sardonic amusement as her cheeks flushed a deep crimson red. 'Alas—I fear my love-life isn't nearly as exciting as you seem to imagine!'

'Hmph!' She gave a scornful laugh. 'Not according to the newspapers. You're always being photographed with one glamorous floozie after another.'

He shrugged his shoulders. 'My dear girl, you really mustn't believe everything you read in the Press.'

Francesca gritted her teeth with frustration at his amused, patronising tone of voice. Trying to expel some of her bad temper—and score a few points off Matt—didn't seem to be working, somehow. The damned man must have a hide like a rhinoceros!

'For instance, if we were to be caught by a sneak photographer right now,' he continued, reaching out a hand to lazily tuck a lock of damp curly blonde hair behind her ear, 'I hate to think of the conclusions some people might draw.'

'That. . .that's ridiculous!' She gave a breathless laugh, unable to prevent an involuntary shiver at his touch.

'Is it?' he drawled, his hand moving slowly down over her bare shoulders. 'I can think of several newspapers which would be very interested in a picture of me with a half-nude—er—floozie!' he added, brushing his fingers lightly across her full breasts.

Francesca jerked backwards, as if she'd been stung. 'Keep your hands off me!' she gasped, quickly grabbing the towel and clutching it tightly to her trembling body.

She could feel herself growing hot with embarrassment and shame. She had, she realised with dawning horror, been so busy trying to quarrel with Matt that she hadn't noticed that her towel had become loose. The question of just how long she'd been sitting there—practically displaying her naked breasts, for heaven's sake!—didn't even bear thinking about. No wonder he hadn't risen to any of her barbed comments.

He'd obviously been far more amused to see her making a complete fool of herself!

Matt's next words confirmed her worst suspicions.

'You didn't like my remarks about your close resemblance to your mother earlier today,' he drawled coldly, 'so—if you don't want other people to draw the some conclusions as myself—I suggest that it's about time you put some clothes on.'

'But I'm only looking like this because you woke me up, thumping your way on to this boat,' she protested angrily. 'I was absolutely exhausted. . .you should have *seen* the mess! So I had a shower, and. . .well, I mean. . .' Her voice trailed away as he lifted a dark, quizzical eyebrow, his eyes sweeping contemptuously over her flushed face and agitated, heated figure.

'There's no need to try and excuse yourself to me,' he remarked flatly. 'I've known you since you were a child—and you're obviously the same silly little girl with loose morals that, unfortunately, I remember only too well!'

'Why, you. . .you. . .'

'I told you *not* to try and do that!' he warned grimly, his hand quickly catching hold of hers as she leaned forward to strike him. 'We none of us like to hear the truth about ourselves,' he grated, his fingers biting cruelly into her soft flesh. 'However, my dear Francesca, don't you think it's about time that you took a good, hard look at yourself?'

'I don't know what you're talking about,' she gasped, wincing with pain as he crushed the fragile bones in her wrist. 'What "truth". . .?'

'I'm talking about the way you seem to have been

living in London over the past few years. Going to all the so-called "smart" parties, and having your picture constantly in the gossip columns—especially with that gormless fool, Rupert ffinch-Rawlings!—is hardly the life your father had hoped or, indeed, planned for you.'

'The "truth" is that you know *nothing* about me—and, apparently, very little about my father,' she panted furiously, finally managing to tear her hand from his clasp. 'Surely you, of all people, must remember that Dad was a supremely selfish, if thoroughly charming man, who only thought about himself? He did care about your mother, of course,' Francesca added quickly. 'But it's no secret that she came a poor second—especially when his own interests were involved.'

'Kindly leave my mother out of this!' he retorted curtly.

'OK. . .' she muttered, 'but it's no good trying to hold my father up to me now as a model of family rectitude. And I'm not too impressed by this "heavy stepbrother" act of yours, either!'

Hard green chips of ice glittered from beneath his hooded eyelids, and her stomach muscles tightened nervously as she noted the angry tension in his clenched jaw. Why did she keep trying to defy this seemingly invincible man?

'Your father made me your legal guardian, and one of your two trustees, until you reach the age of thirty. So, as far as I'm concerned,' Matt declared, his voice hard and implacable, 'I have a right—and a duty—to see that his wishes are carried out. He would not have wanted to see your name, and photographs, appearing regularly in the gutter Press. Nor would he——'

'Hey, just a minute!' she exclaimed angrily. 'I thought *you'd* just told me not to believe everything I read in the newspapers. . .?'

'*Touché*!' he murmured, his lips twisting into a cynical, self-mocking grimace. 'However, the fact remains that you've been receiving a great deal of Press exposure—and I want it to stop.'

'You're unbelievable!' she stormed, clutching the towel tightly to her body as she jumped to her feet and glared down at him. 'If there have been any newspaper reports about me, they will have had to do with gallery openings, and prestigious art shows. As far as I'm concerned, it's good for business—and part of my job. So if you're trying to make out that I'm some sort of blonde bimbo—spending all my time in night-clubs—you. . .you must be out of your mind!' she added with a shrill, high-pitched laugh.

'There's no need to yell at me, Francesca,' he murmured silkily.

'I reckon that I've got a lot to yell about!' she lashed back fiercely. 'I pay a flying visit to Grenada—and before I know what's happening I'm the victim of an *outrageous* confidence trick, find myself dumped on this boat—which was in a quite *disgusting* condition!—and am told that I'm practically a prisoner for the next two weeks. On top of which. . .' her voice rose an octave '. . . I'm now having to listen to a lecture on morals—from a man who's already physically assaulted me!'

'I was under the impression that you'd slapped my

face,' he drawled mockingly. 'I also gained the impression that you enjoyed my—er—assault, hmm?'

'I certainly did *not*!' she snapped furiously as Matt gave a soft, sensual laugh that brought colour flying to her cheeks. 'Just as I'm nothing like my mother. Oh, yes—as you keep reminding me—I *am* Natalie's daughter. So what? I'm not responsible for my birth, am I?' she demanded, trembling with rage.

'I never said that you were,' he pointed out with maddening logic.

'Well, that's just about the only thing you haven't said!' Francesca ground out through clenched teeth. 'Just because I once made a complete and utter fool of myself—I was *only* just sixteen at the time, for heaven's sake!—it doesn't mean that I live a life of loose morals. Didn't you ever do anything stupid when you were very young?'

He gave a harsh, caustic laugh. 'Oh, yes, of course I did. But, I don't remember ever attaining the heights of *your* stupidity!'

'Well—bully for you,' she snapped, seized with an overwhelming longing to kick his shins. Unfortunately, the way her life was going at the moment, she thought glumly, she'd probably only succeed in breaking her toes.

'You were saying. . .?'

'What?' She frowned over at him as his voice cut into her gloomy introspective thoughts.

'I think that I've been remarkably patient,' he remarked blandly, lifting his wrist to look at his watch. 'However, if you've finished ranting and raving about my shortcomings,' he added in a caustic drawl, 'I'd like to go and fetch our supper, which I left on the deck when I heard you screaming about the—er—"monsters".'

She could cheerfully *kill* him! But she'd get her own back somehow, Francesca promised herself grimly.

'As far as your shortcomings are concerned, I haven't even begun to scratch the surface!' she retorted defiantly, before turning to stalk out of the saloon. 'Frankly, Matt, your greatest fault is that you're so *blind* that you aren't capable of recognising the truth—even if it got up and hit you in the face!'

Sitting on the bed in her cabin, half an hour later, Francesca was still burning and trembling with anger. After jumping into a pair of white shorts and a bright pink scooped-neck T-shirt, she'd spent the last thirty minutes rehashing the row with Matt.

Furiously dragging a brush through her unruly long hair, she'd been able to think of some salient remarks and several extremely clever points she could have made. If *only* they'd come to mind when she'd been facing her foul stepbrother! Why was it, she wondered gloomily, that she could always conjure up the perfect *bon mot* only when it was far too late to use it?

However, she had got one thing right—Matt *was* totally blind as far as she was concerned. Not only did he seem to be obsessive about poor Natalie, but there was no way he was ever going to forgive, or forget, what had happened during that family holiday in the South of France all those years ago. The long, hot, seemingly endless summer of the year of her sixteenth birthday, which had found her innocently trembling on the brink of life, and love.

Maybe she had always been in love with Matt. Almost ten years older than herself, he seemed to have moved majestically like a lord through her childhood, carelessly bestowing a friendly pat on the head, or a brief smile, when he'd been home for the holidays. Her stepmother's only child—and clearly the older woman's pride and joy—Matt had never seemed to put a foot wrong. Educated at an English public school, he'd been captain of the cricket team, top of his class in mathematics and the science subjects and when he'd won a scholarship to Cambridge—followed by his post-graduate business course at Harvard—Matt had gained a place in both of those university rowing teams.

Tall, dark and handsome, he had been Francesca's idea of a perfect knight in shining armour, whom she'd always worshipped from afar. And it was to him that she had naturally turned when the whole fabric and substance of her young life had appeared to be falling apart.

Elizabeth Patterson, who'd been the only real mother that Francesca had known, had been clearly ailing for some time. And, when Sir Dennis arranged for his wife and daughter to spend the summer in a large rented villa in the South of France, it was generally agreed that the sun and warmth were just what Elizabeth needed to help her regain her health.

'Why not have one of your school-friends to stay for a while? That girl Paula Gosling, for instance?' her father had suggested. But, like most of his suggestions, it had become an order, despite Francesca's plea that she really didn't like the girl.

'Nonsense—her uncle's a business friend of mine. A

splendid chap,' Sir Dennis had said firmly. 'I'm sure you two girls will get on like a house on fire.'

Unfortunately, they didn't. Paula, a year older than Francesca, with black hair, a sultry face and a curvaceous figure, had proved to be a difficult guest. Thoroughly spoilt by indulgent parents, Paula had quickly become bored, wanting to spend her time away from the villa—preferably in the local bars and discos.

'Don't be so naff!' she'd snapped when Francesca had not wanted to accompany her one night. 'So what if your stepmother wouldn't approve? She doesn't have to know—does she?'

'But La Vivandière is supposed to be an awful place,' Francesca had told her nervously. 'Full of drug barons and. . .and prostitutes!'

'But that's what makes it so exciting!' Paula had giggled. 'Besides, I've already arranged to meet a boy there—he's fixed up one of his friends for you—so we'll have to go.' And, refusing to take no for an answer, she'd bullied the younger girl into going with her.

The low dive was every bit as unpleasant as Francesca had feared it would be. Soon losing contact with Paula in the dimly lit interior, and taking an immediate dislike to the 'friend'—who hadn't seemed able to keep his hands off her—she'd finally managed to escape his clutches by naïvely accepting an offer, from a complete stranger, of a lift in his car back to the villa.

Clearly, her guardian angel had been working overtime. Goodness knew what would have happened to her if she hadn't been able to open the door and escape from the dangerously amorous man when he'd been forced to slow down for a sharp bend. Taking to her heels and running like the wind, she'd eventually arrived back at the villa, her clothes torn, and in a state of complete exhaustion.

As she'd tried to creep into the house and make her way upstairs to her room without being heard, she'd been foiled by the unexpected presence of her step-brother Matt.

'What on earth are you doing here in France? I thought you were still in America,' she'd muttered in confusion, as he'd swept her bedraggled figure up in his arms, carrying her gently up to her room.

'I only arrived an hour ago, but that isn't important,' he'd said impatiently, his brows drawing together in a deep frown at the sight of her torn clothes and bruised body. 'What in the hell's been going on?'

However, as she was clearly too weary and exhausted to go into any details that night, he'd made her promise that she would tell him everything in the morning before helping her to get undressed and into bed.

Unfortunately, Paula had got to him first. By the time Francesca had woken up from a deep sleep, it was to find that the other girl, in order to save her own skin, had neatly and cleverly reversed their roles. It was now *she* and not Paula who had apparently insisted on going to the night-club—despite its evil reputation.

Francesca had still been in her bedroom, trying to disguise some of her bruises, when Matt had found her. She'd blushed nervously when he'd walked in, looking so tall and handsome in blue denims. The dark hairs of his tanned muscular chest beneath the open-necked shirt, and the tight-fitting jeans, hugging the contours of his slim hips and powerful thighs, had sparked a dramatic awareness of him which she hadn't experienced before, her stomach suddenly clenching with a strange mixture of fear and excitement.

Overwhelmed by her first experience of the power of sexual magnetism, she had barely begun to haltingly thank him for his help the previous night when she had realised that he was furiously angry.

'What sort of girl are you?' he demanded angrily. 'You're not stupid. You must have known the sort of dangers you were running by going to such a sordid place. In fact, it's not the first time that you've dragged poor little Paula there, is it?'

'*Paula. . .?*'

'Yes, she tried to be a loyal friend and cover up for you, but I made her tell me the truth,' he ground out, his voice heavy with disgust.

'But. . .but you've got it all wrong!' she cried, convinced that she was in the midst of an appalling nightmare. 'It was Paula who——'

'Don't try and lie your way out of this mess! How *dare* you try and put the blame on your guest—a girl who is clearly innocent?' he'd grated.

'Matt! I haven't done *anything*!' she pleaded tearfully, but he clearly didn't believe her.

'Don't you know that what you've been doing is illegal? That you're still under the age of consent?' He shook his dark head in disbelief. 'I'm only thankful that my mother has no idea of the disgusting promiscuous way you've been behaving these last few weeks.'

'No! No, I haven't!' she cried frantically. 'I'm not like. . .like that!'

'It's obviously a case of history repeating itself,' he told her grimly. 'As far as I can see, you've been behaving *exactly* like your own mother. Natalie has a habit of picking up strange men in night-clubs,' he added, his lips twisting with distaste.

'I've never picked up anyone. . .and I'd never been inside a night-club before last night,' she sobbed helplessly, but his expression remained cold and stern.

'I don't want you running to my mother, snivelling about your problems, either,' he told the young girl savagely. 'All the years she's been married to your father she's had to put up with gossip columns full of Natalie's exploits—each episode more sordid than the last. And now I don't want her worried or upset. Because the reason I've come back here from America is that the doctors say she's very ill with leukaemia.'

'Oh, *no!*' Francesca stared at him through her tears, her blue eyes widening with dawning horror. She might have been ignorant of sexual matters, but she was quite able to comprehend what he was saying: that her beloved stepmother didn't have very long to live.

When she tried, yet again, to explain what had really happened the previous night, he wouldn't even listen to her.

'Just keep out of my sight!' he'd warned her grimly, before leaving the room and slamming the door loudly behind him.

Mercifully, Matt had used the excuse of his mother's illness to put Paula on the plane back to London the following day. And if Francesca—who'd refused point-blank to see or talk to her so-called friend before she'd left—had hoped for divine retribution, even she couldn't have foreseen the speed with which it had taken place. A bare three months after her departure from France, Paula had been apprehended, along with some other rich young friends, at a drink and drugs party.

There had been huge headlines in the English Press, carrying full reports of the latest scandal which had also involved the sons and daughters of some British politicians. But by then it was far too late to mend matters. The damage between herself and Matt had already been done.

As Elizabeth Patterson's life had drawn slowly to its close, Francesca had drifted like a wraith around the silent house and grounds. Since his wife had wanted to spend her last days in the wramth of the Mediterranean, Sir Dennis was temporarily running his business from the villa, and had had little or no time to spare for his daughter. Other than her brief daily visits to her stepmother's room, and an occasional word from her deeply worried father, she had done her best to keep out of everyone's way—especially avoiding all contact with Matt.

The night following her stepmother's death had seemed endless. Her father had locked himself away in his study, and Matt seemed to have completely disappeared. Francesca, totally devastated and grief-stricken by her loss, had not been able to find relief in sleep. Tossing and turning through the interminable hours of that hot, humid night, she'd eventually given up the struggle. Sitting curled up on the window-seat of her bedroom, gazing out at the garden lit by the eerie silvery glow of brilliant moonlight, she'd been overwhelmed by despair and deep unhappiness.

And it was there that Matt had eventually found her. Drawn to her room by the sound of muffled sobs, he'd discovered the young girl distraught and shaken by a storm of desolate tears. Softly murmuring her name, he'd walked across the room, sitting down beside her and quietly gathering her weeping figure to his arms.

The warmth of his embrace had been almost more than she could bear. She knew that he, too, was in dire need of comfort, and she'd instinctively clasped him tightly to her, cradling his dark head on her breasts.

Francesca never really knew at what point during that long silent embrace the simple need for mutual consolation gradually became something very different. It was some time before she became aware that Matt's skin was damp from a recent shower, and that on this stifling hot night he was wearing nothing but a light towel about his waist. His body was hard and firm, and she could feel the warmth of his bare muscular chest through her flimsy silk nightgown.

Shafts of silver moonlight, streaming in through the open window, covered their still figures in a strange glow. Bemused by the dream-like atmosphere, she gently stroked his thick dark hair, her hands, almost of their own volition, trailing down to softly touch his bronzed shoulder-blades with her fingertips. Gently she moved them across his back, her feather-light touch producing a deep, muffled groan as he pressed his lips to the soft curve of her breast, his arms tightening about her quivering body.

Having no idea of the forces she had so innocently released, Francesca trembled with a need and desire that was impossible to deny. And it had seemed as if he, too, was suddenly overwhelmed by the same raw hunger, lifting his head and possessing her lips with an urgency that swept aside all past barriers.

Her emotions completely out of control, she shivered and moaned in delight as his fingers roughly brushed aside the thin straps of her gown, his lips moving down to kiss the soft creamy flesh of her breasts.

'I love you!' she gasped as his mouth and tongue moved enticingly over her aroused, swollen pink nipples. She had never known such exquisite agony, never dreamed that she could find herself drowning in a dark shimmering pool of such rampant desire. 'Oh, Matt—I love you with all my heart!'

It must have been her husky cries of delight which broke through his own passionate response. Because he seemed to freeze in her arms, and then, with shocking suddenness, he almost threw her from him.

'My God—what am I doing? I must be out of my mind!' he cried hoarsely, swiftly rising to his feet and backing away from her trembling figure as if she carried some evil disease.

Totally bemused, and still locked in a thick web of newly awakened passion and desire, she wasn't able to comprehend what was happening to her.

'But. . .but I love you,' she cried, heedless of her silk gown slithering down to the floor as she jumped up, before running to throw her thin arms about him.

'I've always loved you. . .ever since I can remember. . .'

'What do you know of love? You're Natalie's daughter, aren't you?' he snarled, pushing her violently away. 'And, for goodness' sake, cover yourself up!'

Francesca flinched beneath the disgust in his eyes, clearly visible in the bright moonlight. Whimpering with bewilderment, she retrieved her nightgown, clutching it to her body, which still trembled and shook with unfulfilled desire.

'I. . . I don't understand,' she moaned pitiously. 'I thought you loved me too. You've just been kissing me, and. . .and. . .' She blushed a fiery red, trembling as she recalled the exciting, wonderfully entrancing way he'd kissed her lips and her body.

'I can only imagine that I must have been completely moonstruck!' he hissed savagely. 'You've cast some weird, silvery spell over me—just as you've obviously done to all those other men you've slept with!'

She gazed at him in bewilderment. 'But. . .but I don't know any other men. And I've never——'

'You're not even sixteen!'

'Yes, I am—almost. My birthday is next week, and. . .'

Matt groaned heavily, brushing his hands roughly through his thick dark hair. 'Don't you *know* what you've been doing?'

'I. . . I know that I do truly love you, Matt,' she said, taking her courage in both hands and staring him straight in the face. 'I can't help being much. . .much younger than you, but if you'd just wait a bit I'll soon grow up. And then we can get married, and. . .'

'And live happily ever after. . .?' He gave a cruel laugh. 'No—thank you! Natalie's daughter is the very *last* woman I'd ever marry. However, since my own mother is dead,' he added harshly, 'I don't need to have anything more to do with either you or your father. So keep well away from me, Francesca. Not only do I never want to see you again, but if I ever do—believe me, you will be *very* sorry!'

Francesca had practically collapsed when he had left the room, his cruel rebuttal of her love causing her as much if not more pain than her stepmother's death. The two incidents fusing together in her distraught mind had given her dreadful nightmares for years afterwards.

The confrontation with Matt had, however, had one salutary effect. It had successfully killed any desire that she might have had to experiment with her own sexuality. As she'd grown up, and realised that her feelings for Matt had been the stuff of pure fairy-tale romances, she'd also been careful not to get too close to any of her boyfriends. Never again would she allow herself to become so vulnerable, to expose her deepest emotions to the sort of cruel rejection that she had experienced at the hands of Matthew Sinclair.

Francesca had only seen him once in the last eight years—at her father's funeral, held at a church in the City of London. On that occasion, although he had merely given her a curt nod, she'd been acutely conscious of his hard green eyes staring fixedly at her throughout the service.

No wonder she'd been terrified of meeting him again! Francesca thought grimly, coming back to the present

with a jerk as she heard a loud knock on the cabin
door.

'Supper's ready.'

'Go away!' she called out, determined to stay well
away from Matt, even if she was hungry enough to eat
a horse.

'If you don't open this door immediately—I'll break
it down!' he threatened.

It didn't need the determined note in his voice to tell
her that he was quite capable of doing so.

'Oh, all right—I'm coming,' she muttered bitterly.
On her way across the small cabin she caught sight of
her reflection in a mirror fixed to the wall. Hang in
there—it's only going to be for two weeks! she
mouthed silently at herself.

But, unfortunately, the blue eyes staring back at her
didn't look at all confident. They clearly had severe
doubts and dire misgivings about her ability to endure
the next fourteen days.

CHAPTER FOUR

FRANCESCA glared up at the man towering over her. His tall, muscular frame seemed to fill the open doorway of her cabin. And, as always, when in proximity to Matt, she found herself feeling intimidated and vulnerable.

'I'm only coming out of here on two conditions,' she announced breathlessly.

'Oh, really. . .?' he drawled, raising a dark sardonic eyebrow. 'I don't think you're in a position to dictate terms to me, do you? All I have to do is put you over my shoulder, and——'

'Don't you dare!' she gasped, backing nervously away from his dominating figure.

Matt sighed impatiently. 'I was merely pointing out that I'm obviously much stronger than you are. However, far from wishing to initiate any strong-arm tactics, I'm only asking you to join me for supper. To tell you the truth, Francesca—I'm starving!'

'Well. . .' she hesitated for a moment, her tense figure gradually relaxing beneath the warmth of his surprisingly friendly smile '. . .well. . . OK—just as long as you don't make any more snide comments regarding my mother, or about my clothes.'

'Believe me,' he grinned, 'I'm far too interested in food to worry about anything else at the moment.' He shrugged his shoulders. 'However, if it makes you feel any better I'll promise to leave Natalie off the menu.'

'And no caustic comments about what I'm wearing?' she added stubbornly.

His green eyes flicked quickly over her figure-hugging T-shirt and the brief pair of shorts over her long, slim legs. The beautiful, shy and withdrawn little girl that he'd once known had now clearly become a very beautiful and desirable woman. However, since she was also proving to be extremely prickly and difficult, this was probably *not* the moment to say so. And especially not if he was hoping to eat any supper tonight, he reminded himself with grim amusement.

'Well?' Francesca demanded.

'I can't think why you feel there's a problem,' he murmured smoothly. 'You look perfectly all right to me.'

'Well, that's a mercy,' she muttered sarcastically. 'Because I don't have any other clothes to put on.' Gazing glumly down at her white shorts and pink T-shirt, she continued, 'I thought I'd only be here in the Caribbean for two days at the most. However, after my scrubbing out this boat, the things I had on this morning are going to need a good soaking in disinfectant! The only other garment I've got is a silk dress, for dining in the hotel, so. . .'

Matt groaned. 'Why are women always yacking on about their clothes? All right!' he added hastily, raising his hands in mock-surrender as she scowled up at him. 'I'll arrange for you to go shopping first thing tomorrow morning. Charge anything you need to use.'

'Anything. . .?'

'You can buy up the whole of St George's, as far as I'm concerned,' he said brusquely. 'Now—is that all?'

She shook her head. 'No, it's not. I've had a long, exhausting day, and the last thing I need is another row. So I want you to promise that there won't be any more arguments.'

'Oh, Francesca—what an idiot you are!' He gave a soft, taunting laugh which sent nervous shivers down her backbone. 'You know very well that you were dying to pick a quarrel with me, right from the moment I came aboard this boat.'

She felt her cheeks growing hot and flushed. Did the damn man *always* have to keep trying to win every point?

'There you go again!' she muttered with a heavy sigh, staring blindly down at her bare feet. 'Honestly, Matt, I'm fed up to the back teeth with your continually pointing out my defects. Why can't we have an ordinary, pleasant meal, without fighting with one another?' she added plaintively.

'Why not, indeed?' he agreed smoothly, putting a surprisingly gentle hand on her arm, and leading her reluctant figure down the passageway towards the saloon.

'That was a really terrific meal,' Francesca told him some time later, sighing happily as she leaned back against the cushions of the upholstered dining seat, which formed an L-shape behind the large table at the end of the saloon, adjacent to the galley.

However much she'd dreaded having to join Matt for supper, she had been relieved to discover that her

fears had been groundless. Clearly setting out to be a
charming host, Matt had confined his conversation to
the lighter, more amusing and interesting aspects of his
life, allowing her a glimpse into the other side of his
hard, formidable character. Francesca had been surprised and impressed, for instance, to learn that Matt
had sailed *Silver Lady* in the two-handed Transatlantic
Race, taking only thirteen days to cross the Atlantic
Ocean.

'When I'm tired of life in New York, or feel like
some respite from business—I leave it all behind and
go sailing,' he'd told her, which explained why he was
abandoning his large motor yacht for the next two
weeks. It was, apparently, mainly used as a floating
office while he was away from New York.

Although she'd tried hard to resist the force of his
charm, Francesca had been unable to prevent herself
from succumbing to the overwhelming impact of his
magnetic personality. It wouldn't last, of course. They
were bound, sooner or later, to find themselves in the
middle of yet another major quarrel. But, sitting here
in the soft candlelight, vibrantly aware of the glinting
green eyes beneath their heavy, sensual lids, conveying
the surprising but unmistakable message that he found
her an attractive woman—anything seemed possible.
Cradled within the gently rocking boat, the surrounding warm darkness of the Caribbean night pierced by
the soft, twinkling lights of the boats and the houses
surrounding the bay, it was tempting to imagine that
they might be able to forget the traumas of the past.

However, there was no point in trying to deceive
herself. She knew that it was a foolish dream—a

beguiling, insidious fantasy which could lead to nothing but grief and unhappiness. Too much had happened, too many things had been said and done for either of them to recapture the easy, carefree relationship which they had once enjoyed, so long ago.

In fact, she really ought not to drink any more, she quickly reminded herself as Matt topped up her glass with sparkling champagne. She must try to keep all her wits about her. Because, however attractive and charming he might appear on the surface, she would do well to remember that the central core of this dangerous man was composed of nothing but hard, cold steel.

'How about some more chocolate mousse?'

'Oh, no—I couldn't possibly manage another mouthful! But you can tell Pierre that I'm prepared to forgive him for refusing to work on this boat,' she said with a light laugh. 'Anyone who can produce that sort of meal is a genius!'

Matt took a sip from his glass. 'Hmm. . .it wasn't bad.'

'You must be joking!' she exclaimed. 'As far as I'm concerned, those red snapper fillets in avocado and lime sauce were just out of this world!'

'I'm sure they'll pale in comparison to the meals you'll be providing during the next two weeks,' he drawled silkily.

Francesca gave a gurgle of laughter. 'Now I *know* you're joking! To tell you the truth, I'm just keeping my fingers crossed, and hoping that no one is expecting too much—and certainly not *haute cuisine*. Which reminds me,' she added, 'who exactly are you expecting on this boat tomorrow?'

'An old friend, Benjamin Wagner, plus his wife and young daughter. You'll like Ben,' Matt told her. 'He was a great pal of my father's—they went to college together—and, now that he's retired and sold off his large real-estate business, he's thinking of buying himself a yacht.'

'So he's joining you to see if he likes sailing?'

Matt grinned. 'No, not entirely. He's already sold on the idea of owning his own boat. However, I gather that Ben is hoping to persuade his wife that it's a good idea. She's much younger than he is, and would apparently prefer to buy a large house in Palm Beach.'

'Ah—so *that's* why I've suddenly found myself drafted into this job. Clearly, it's *Mrs* Wagner who has to be kept happy and well-fed. . .right?'

'Absolutely right!' he laughed. 'Gloria can be—er— just a little difficult at times, and, for Ben's sake, I want this cruise to be a success. Oh, by the way,' he added as an afterthought, 'it would probably be better if we don't mention that we are related to one another in any way.'

She gave him a puzzled glance. 'That's all right by me,' she shrugged. 'Incidentally, I was relieved to see that fridge in the galley. I had dreadful visions of everyone going down with ptomaine poisoning!'

'Relax—there's no need to worry. You'll be fine.'

'Matt! Are you sure you're feeling all right?' She grinned at him. 'This foolish optimism doesn't sound like you.'

'No, you're right—it doesn't!' he agreed with a laugh.

'So what's happened to the grim dark ogre we all love to hate?' she asked carelessly, before quickly wishing that she'd kept her mouth shut.

Although he was now regarding her with a blank expression, she'd caught the brief, chilling glint in his green eyes before it was quickly masked by his heavy eyelids. 'Is that really how you see me, Francesca?' he asked quietly.

'I. . . I suppose that was unfair of me, in a way. . .' she muttered nervously, realising that it might have been a mistake to have drunk quite so much champagne. 'I mean, I don't really know anything about you, do I?'

'Don't you. . .?'

'No—how could I? We've seen nothing of each other for the past eight years. In fact, this is the first time we've spent any time together since—er—since your mother died. . .' Her voice trailed away as she stared down at her empty plate. 'You probably won't believe me, but hardly a day goes by without my thinking about Elizabeth—and how much I miss her,' Francesca added huskily.

'I know. I miss her too,' he murmured with a sigh. 'However, she'd be the last person to want us sitting here, indulging in gloomy retrospection,' he added firmly.

'Yes, you're right,' Francesca agreed, giving him a shaky smile. 'She'd certainly be highly amused to know that I'm going to be cooking for you, and your guests, during the next fortnight. Your mother used to tease me about being so undomesticated—forecasting that when I grew up I'd be completely useless in a kitchen!'

Matt shrugged his broad shoulders. 'You were only a child. A lot of water has passed under the bridge since then.'

'Yes, and that's what I was saying earlier. I honestly didn't mean to—er—say the wrong thing,' she told him earnestly. 'But it *is* true that I don't really know you—just as you seem to know very little about me. I mean. . .' she paused, taking a deep breath as she tried to ignore the alcohol fumes clouding her normally clear brain, and concentrate on explaining the problem. '. . .it's been years and years since we've exchanged more than a brief word, right?' She continued, feeling encouraged as he remained silent, 'So if our characters hadn't altered or changed, if we hadn't learned something from life during that time, we'd both be very peculiar people. I mean, you must be about thirty-two or three now. . .'

'Thirty-four.'

'There you are—I wasn't even sure about that! And although I know you're a successful, rich entrepreneur, widely feared by your business rivals—that's only what I've gleaned from the newspapers.' She grimaced slightly. 'And even you yourself warned me earlier today not to believe everything I read in the Press.'

'And just what do you want to know?' Matt enquired smoothly.

'Well. . . I can't help wondering what *really* makes you tick. Why you seem to have such a compulsive urge to win. And. . .and I know nothing about your current likes and dislikes—the sort of books you read, for instance, or the type of music you prefer. And there are lots of other items. . .' She paused, frowning for a moment. 'Good heavens! I've just realised that I don't even know if you're married. . .'

'My dear Francesca—I had no idea you were *so* interested in me,' he drawled with heavy sarcasm, his gaze narrowing as he continued to regard her with an otherwise blank expression on his handsome face.

'I'm not,' she snapped, nettled by his patronising tone. 'But I do know one thing: I'll never again make the mistake of signing a contract with you—not without a battery of lawyers at my side!'

Matt raised a dark, supercilious eyebrow. 'But surely you would regard that as learning—er—"something from life", which seemed to form part of your lecture just now?'

'I wasn't lecturing,' Francesca protested. Why did this hateful man always seem to twist everything she said? 'I was just trying to point out that we've both changed—and that I don't know much about you. Other than the fact that you're a double-crossing rat!' she added grimly.

'You signed the agreement—so it's too late to complain now. Besides, I thought we'd agreed not to quarrel?' he murmured, a hard note of warning in his voice.

'Yes, we did.' She gazed stormily at him. 'But I didn't agree to sit here and have to listen to your being so damned condescending! Which reminds me: maybe I *do* know something else about you, after all.'

'Oh, yes?'

'Well, it's more of an inspired guess, of course.' She

gave him a tight, malicious grin. 'Still, I'd lay any money on the fact that you're not married. Or, if you once were married, that you've now been divorced.'

He stared at her silently for a minute. 'All right—I'll buy it,' he said at last. 'Why are you so certain?'

When she thought about the incident later Francesca could see that the champagne had *definitely* gone to her head. But, at the time, she was so pleased with herself for having found *the* perfect squelch—that she foolishly disregarded all prudence and caution.

Raising her glass, she threw him a wide beaming smile, which she hoped he would find extremely irritating.

'I'm certain that you aren't married because—if my own experience today is anything to go by—you clearly regard women as a sub-species of the human race,' she told him sweetly. 'So it's obvious, my dear Matt, that no woman—and definitely not one in her right mind!—is going to sign on for life with such a male chauvinist pig!'

As Francesca laughed, before tipping the contents of the glass down her throat, she heard his quick indrawn breath. Even without looking at him, she knew that he was furious. Good! It wouldn't do him any harm to have to listen to a few home truths for a change. Eight years ago she'd been too young to defend herself. But now things were going to be very different.

'There speaks a woman scorned!' he rasped angrily.

'A. . .a *what*?' she gasped, almost choking on her champagne as she tried to comprehend what he was saying. Surely even Matt couldn't seriously think that she was still in love with him?

'Not only have you obviously drunk far too much,' he said coldly as he removed the glass from her fingers, 'but it's equally obvious that you've never forgiven me for turning you down.'

'You. . .you *must* be out of your mind! And if you think that I'm going to sit here, listening to any more of this nonsense. . .' she told him, trying to get out from behind the table—not an easy task, since it was firmly anchored to the carpeted floor of the boat.

'You'll stay—until I say you can go!' he grated angrily, his hand snaking out to catch hold of her arm.

'*Ouch*! What do you think you're doing?' she cried, bewildered and confused to find herself being jerked forcefully back along the cushioned bench towards his tall, dominant figure.

'It's about time you grew up and learned some manners!' he growled, staring down at her grimly. 'If you'd bothered to ask me—instead of giving vent to childish verbal abuse—I could have told you that I am about to become engaged to a very beautiful girl.'

'Oh—well—er—that's great. Congratulations,' she muttered, far more interested in trying to wrest her arm away from his tight clasp than in his matrimonial plans.

'However, it's obvious that you've always carried a torch for me,' he continued, ignoring her words. 'And now—when I'm still clearly not interested—you're reduced to making infantile assumptions about my lifestyle.'

'*Me*. . .? Still carrying a torch for you?' she screeched incredulously before giving a shrill laugh.

'*You must be out of your mind*! Believe me—if I was that desperate, I'd shoot myself!'

'Oh, yes. . .?' he sneered.

Francesca could feel herself sobering up fast as she realised that he really *was* serious. She felt stifled and dominated by his sheer size, every instinct screaming at her to get away from this dangerous man as quickly as possible. But she had virtually no room for manoeuvre, tightly confined by both the table—which was clearly immovable—and the fact that Matt clearly didn't intend to let her escape.

'I might have been stupid enough to think I was in love with you when I was only sixteen,' she said, despising herself for not being able to hide the wobbly tremor in her voice, 'but that was *years* ago. The girl you once knew no longer exists—except, perhaps, in your overheated imagination. And. . .and you don't seem to have the first idea about the woman she's become!' she added defiantly.

Then maybe it's time I began to find out,' he drawled mockingly, his green eyes glinting with cruel intent as he pulled her closer to his tall, muscular figure.

'Let me go, Matt!' she raged, struggling to wriggle free of his iron grip. 'What are you trying to prove? I. . . I don't feel *anything* for you. Not now. . .!' she panted breathlessly.

'Don't you?' he murmured cynically, quickly pushing her agitated figure back against the cushions, his superior weight pinning her down beneath the hard male warmth of his body.

'*No!*' she cried hoarsely, determined to defy him to her last gasp, although she knew it was hopeless when she felt his long tanned fingers burying themselves in her cloud of pale silvery hair. Her brain seemed to be throbbing with a strange fever as the grip of his fingers tightened, tilting her head back so that she was forced to look up into his face. Her eyes widened in alarm, her pulses raced with fear and trepidation as she gazed helplessly at the cruel, sensual line of his mouth, not an ounce of mercy in those stony, hard emerald-green eyes.

'*I hate you!*' she moaned as his dark head came down towards her, his mouth trailing across her cheek in a feather-light caress, hovering tantalisingly over her quivering lips. She watched its inevitable downward movement like an animal transfixed by the headlamps of a car, her muscles taut as a bow-string, even her breathing suspended for one heart-stopping moment.

'Hate? Oh, no—I don't think you hate me, Francesca,' he breathed huskily, sliding his tongue delicately over her trembling lips. 'In fact, I'm very sure that you still want me.'

'No!' she sobbed, but the sound was lost, obliterated by the cruel pressure of his mouth forcing her lips open to allow him to ravage the softness within. She was unable to move. Held so tightly and forcefully beneath him, she was aware of every muscle and fibre in his powerful body. His kiss seemed unending, and she was almost in tears when the pressure of his mouth gradually eased, and she trembled as his lips became soft and seductive, igniting an answering flame deep inside her.

Shamefully, she appeared helpless to resist a response that seemed to arise of its own accord; a fierce excitement which filled her entire being. A slow, pulsing ache began to throb deep in her stomach as he once more teased her quivering lips lightly open, and unconsciously she arched herself against him. Her arms clung weakly to his shoulders, her senses spinning out of control as a hot storm of desire roared through every fibre of her being.

There was no thought to deny him as his hands moved enticingly over her body, a moan breaking from her throat as his fingers slid beneath her T-shirt, expertly releasing the front fastening of her bra to free the creamy fullness of her breasts.

An explosive tension was mounting deep inside her, fuelled, it seemed, by a flame that had never really died. But now it was a far darker, more fiercely raging fire that had little to do with her pure virginal emotions of eight years ago. She had never before experienced this wanton need to touch his body as he was touching hers, nor the driving compulsion to respond to the ever-increasing pleasure and excitement spiralling through her veins. Her nostrils were filled with the delicious musky scent of his male body, each nerve-end in her breasts tingling as the rosy nipples became hard and swollen beneath the delicate mastery of his touch.

Matt was right, she realised with despair. This was what he'd deliberately set out to prove. He meant her to feel like this—to acknowledge the fact that she still wanted him. And then she was lost, mindless, moaning softly as his lips trailed slowly down the long line of her throat. Her heart pounded like a sledge-hammer as he lifted her towards him, his lips and tongue teasing first one exposed, erect nipple and then the other, brief inarticulate moans of pleasure breaking from her as she was carried along on a tide of sensuality so intense that she felt as though she was drowning in ecstasy.

While she was caught up in a mad frenzy of desire, her burning flesh on fire for his touch, it didn't seem to matter that she was being betrayed by her errant emotions. It was no longer of any importance, not when her whole existence was now focused on the sensations churning deep inside her, an ancient, primitive need and desire for this man's possession.

And then, with shocking suddenness, she was free, her confused mind barely registering the muffled sound of Matt swearing savagely as he pushed her roughly away from him. There was a long silence, only broken by the sound of Matt's harsh, laboured breathing as he rose to his feet. Francesca's dazed eyes tried to focus on the tall figure staring down at her with fiercely glittering eyes, a muscle beating wildly in his tightly clenched jaw.

'*Quod erat demonstrandum*—or QED—as my old Latin master used to say.' Matt's deep, husky tones seemed to echo eerily around the confined space of the saloon. 'However, to put it in plain English: I think I've proved my point—don't you?'

Weak with shock, and shuddering from the maelstrom of emotions which his lovemaking had released, Francesca remained lying helplessly against the cushions for a moment. Unable to speak, barely able even to move any of her limbs, which seemed to have been turned to lead, she eventually found the strength to sit up. Her face flaming with embarrassment, she hurriedly adjusted her clothing before inching her way along to the end of the bench and staggering towards a nearby settee.

Trembling like a leaf, she collapsed down on to the cushions, desperately trying to pull herself together. The passion and desire of a few moments ago was now slowly draining away, and, despite the heat of the hot Caribbean night, she was left shivering with cold misery and despair.

'Here—you'd better drink this.'

The oddly constrained, tense voice seemed to be coming from somewhere far away. It was only when Matt lifted one of her limp hands, carefully placing a brandy glass between her shaking fingers, that she could begin to face the reality of her situation. Staring blindly down at the clear amber liquid in the glass, Francesca would have given everything she possessed to be able to sink right through the bottom of this boat, down into the cold, inky blue-black darkness of the Caribbean Sea.

'Are you all right?' Matt asked quietly.

Slowly raising her head, she gazed with loathing at the man who was clearly the architect of her misfortunes. How dared he stand there, leaning casually against the wooden frame of the bar, idly sipping his brandy as if he hadn't a care in the world?

'If I didn't need this drink I'd throw it in your face!' she answered bitterly, her voice, even to her own ears, sounding hoarse and shaken.

'Francesca. I. . .' He paused, thrusting a hand roughly through his thick dark hair.

'Please. . .please just go away, and leave me alone,' she muttered helplessly, cringing with embarrassment beneath the hard, icy green eyes staring at her so fixedly.

'Don't be ridiculous,' he snapped curtly. 'I can't possibly leave you in this state.'

'Why not? You deliberately set out to put me in "this state", as you call it,' she ground out savagely, her teeth clattering nervously against the side of her glass. She normally hated the taste of brandy, but now she was finding it a help in combating the shock waves of shame and humiliation pounding through her trembling body.

'Is this how you get your kicks, Matt?' she continued, wanting to hit out at the man who'd caused her so much anguish. 'Is it your usual practice to force yourself on a woman, however unwilling she might be?'

'My God—*no*!' he exploded angrily.

'Then why. . .?' she cried, raising a trembling hand to her head, which was beginning to throb with a dull ache. 'What have I ever done that could possibly——'

His harsh, mirthless bark of laughter cut cruelly across her words. 'It isn't so much what you've done— although that was bad enough—it's what you *are*!' he ground out savagely. 'You're a spoilt little rich girl, Francesca, and everything you've ever wanted has always been instantly available to you. So I was merely proving to you that there are *some* things you cannot have, and at the moment—I'm one of them!'

'You. . .you egotistical bastard!' she hissed, outrage at being used to demonstrate some crazy whim of his rapidly taking over from the embarrassment and shocked dismay she felt about her own behaviour.

'And you obviously haven't changed your ways,' he

told her grimly, apparently not in the least affected by her bowed shoulders and ashen face. 'That simple-minded fool, Rupert ffinch-what's-his-name, may not care about all the other men in your life, but *I* wouldn't dream of sullying myself with second-hand goods!'

'There are no other men in my life,' she muttered dully. 'And I can't think why you're dragging poor Rupert into this.'

'"Poor Rupert" hasn't just been your constant companion for the past two years—I understand that he's now moved into your flat in London, hmm?'

'Yes, he has,' she mumbled wearily, swept by a deep longing to be able to put her head down and go to sleep for a week. 'So what?'

'So if he's now your live-in lover I'd be fascinated to hear how you're going to manage to fit in all your other boyfriends,' Matt taunted.

Francesca's jaw dropped. What on earth was he talking about? And then, at the thought of having Rupert for a lover, she couldn't help giving a brief, hysterical bark of laughter.

'I'm glad you can find something funny about your disgusting behaviour,' he grated angrily.

'I don't,' she snapped, 'only the fact that you seem to see me as some sort of scarlet woman. Besides. . .what happened just now. . .it wasn't all one-sided, was it?' she accused him bleakly. 'I may have temporarily lost my mind—but it was pretty obvious that you too—er—I mean. . .'

'If you're trying to say that I find you very attractive—you're quite correct, I do,' he rasped. 'However, it's also correct to say that I could have had you. . .just like *that*!' he clicked his fingers contemptuously.

Francesca shuddered, burying her face in her hands for a moment as fresh waves of chagrin and misery scorched through her tired figure.

'I'm glad to see that you're not bothering to deny the fact,' he sneered. Blanching as his cruel taunt echoed around the room, she managed to force herself to her feet, walking past Matt on legs that seemed to tremble convulsively with every step. He moved quickly to intercept her, gazing intently at her chalky-white exhausted face.

'Just where do you think you're going?'

'I'm going to bed,' she muttered listlessly. 'You can break my door down, jump all over me with hobnailed boots or take a running jump into the Caribbean Sea. Quite frankly, Matt, I'm simply too dog-tired to care *what* you do.'

He put a hand on her arm. 'Francesca, I can't let you——'

'Goodnight, Matt,' she murmured, brushing him aside as she stumbled out of the room towards her cabin. Opening the door, she threw herself down on to the bed, and a few seconds later she had fallen exhausted into a deep, dreamless sleep.

CHAPTER FIVE

FRANCESCA was woken the next morning by the sound of a heavy fist pounding on her cabin door. It seemed to echo exactly the painful throbbing beat in her head, she thought, groaning as she raised her tired, muzzy head from the pillow.

'Hey there—rise and shine!' Calvin called out as she struggled to wind a thin cotton sheet about her body.

'I. . . I'll be with you in a minute,' she croaked, wincing as the words seemed to reverberate noisily in her brain.

'It looks as if you've got the mother and father of all hangovers!' Calvin told her some minutes later as she sat huddled on a stool in the galley. 'I guess you'd better get this down you—real quick,' he added, handing her a mug of hot black coffee.

'Umm. . .' she mumbled, giving him a brief, pitiful attempt at a smile. 'I feel like death,' she added, her hands shaking as she raised the mug to her lips.

'Yeah, you don't look too good. I guess you and the boss really hit the bottle last night,' Calvin said with a smile. 'I ain't never seen Mr Sinclair the worse for drink—but he sure is in one hell of a temper this morning! So I reckon it would be a smart move to keep well out of his way!'

Francesca flinched as Calvin's bellow of laughter reverberated around the small galley. 'Yes—er—that sounds like a good idea,' she muttered, almost bursting into tears as she realised that, if she hadn't made the stupid mistake of coming out to see Matt, here in Grenada, she could have been safely tucked up in her flat in London.

However, by the time she was on her third mug of black coffee, Francesca was beginning to think that she might—possibly—be going to live, after all. The heavy jangling in her head seemed to have steadied down into a dull ache, her slightly more optimistic mood helped by Calvin's announcement that 'the boss' had sent him over to take her shopping.

'He says you need a *whole* lot of new clothes,' Calvin declared, handing her the white shorts and pink T-shirt that she'd been wearing the previous night.

Francesca stared bemusedly down at the garments—which appeared to have been freshly washed and ironed. Unfortunately, she couldn't seem to recall what had happened after she'd left Matt in the saloon last night. She did have a vague recollection of throwing herself, fully dressed, down on to the bed in her cabin. And, while she knew she hadn't been feeling too good—who was she kidding? She'd felt *awful!*—her fuddled brain simply couldn't seem to work out how her clothes could have been laundered, and returned to her, in such a short space of time.

The thought of Matt undressing her was too hideous to contemplate! Her cheeks flushed a fiery red as she tried to think of some other explanation. If not he, then who. . .? And how. . .?

Her agonised thoughts were interrupted as Calvin said, 'If you wants to do some clothes shopping we'd

better get a move on. I gotta take the boss to the
airport in a couple of hours' time to meet these people
he's got coming from the States. So let's hit the town,
huh?'

Francesca, despite all those mugs of liquid caffeine,
was still feeling slightly displaced; when she and Calvin
arrived along side of the jetty, in St George's, it was as
if her head was somehow not properly attached to her
body. So perhaps that was the reason why, after Calvin
had tied up the dinghy and helped her ashore, she'd
proceeded to throw all prudence and caution to the
winds.

Fuelled by an all-consuming rage against the man
who was casting such a blight on her life, she quickly
decided that she might as well be hung for a sheep as a
lamb. Since her hateful stepbrother seemed determined
to regard her as a promiscuous, spoilt little rich girl—
she might as well act the part! And, discovering that
Matt Sinclair's name seemed to be a golden passport,
she proceeded to rush from one boutique to another,
ordering anything which took her fancy—and a few
outrageous outfits, best viewed by those with a strong
stomach and wearing large dark glasses.

Even Calvin felt compelled to question one purchase. 'Wow-ee!' he laughed, as she held up a dress
smothered in dazzling silver and gold sequins. 'The
boss ain't going to be too crazy about *that* little
number!' he warned, rolling his eyes at the minimal
bodice, which seemed to consist of merely two brief
scraps of material.

'Less is more!' she told him with an hysterical giggle,

before adding the garment to a large heap of parcels he was carrying.

However, by the time she'd finished her mad shopping spree, and Calvin had taken her back to the yacht, Francesca was in a decidedly more sober mood. It was too late now to wish that she hadn't behaved quite so badly. But, despite Matt's provocation, she could now see that she'd been indulging in a very childish form of defiance. Although her stepbrother could well afford it, she'd never really had any intention of wearing that utterly revolting dress. Even telling herself that she'd only bought the horrid thing because she hoped Matt would be furious when he saw her in it didn't seem to excuse her crazy action. Grimacing at her own folly, she quickly bundled the dress up and hid it away in the back of a locker.

Trying to think what to give everyone for lunch, Francesca found herself in an angony of indecision. And not just about the meal. What on earth was she going to say to Matt? What *could* she possibly say after their disastrous confrontation the previous evening? *Plus* the fact that she was now certain it must have been Matt who had removed the clothes from her comatose body. Leaving aside the acute embarrassment she felt whenever she thought about the incident, it *definitely* wasn't the sort of kind, considerate action that one would expect from such a tough man.

Her face burned as she desperately tried not to remember how easily—and fatally—she'd melted in his arms. What was wrong with her, for heaven's sake? Why was it that, despite hating the awful man, she still seemed to go to pieces whenever she was near him?

Although she'd tried to think of a good rational explanation for her peculiar behaviour she hadn't had much success. It was no good even pretending that it had anything to do with her past childish fantasies about him. Unfortunately, she was under no illusions that her instinctive emotional response to Matt's love-making had been anything other than an adult one. Even now, after all those brutally unkind, contentious words of scorn which he'd poured over her head, she still seemed to feel weak at the knees whenever she thought about the odious man.

Desperately trying to ignore such words as 'lust', 'desire' and 'passion', Francesca tried to concentrate on preparing lunch. But she seemed unable to throw off her deep sense of fear and trepidation—particularly about what she was going to say, or do, when Matt and his guests arrived on the yacht.

In the event, she needn't have worried. The appearance of the Wagners—together with the constant toing and froing of small boats between Matt's larger yacht *Wall Street II* and *Silver Lady*—meant that she and Matt had, thankfully, little or no opportunity to say anything to each other. Especially since Francesca's full attention was concentrated on the two female members of the party: Gloria and Lois Wagner.

Gloria Wagner was a small, fiendishly thin woman of goodness knew what age—since she was clearly fighting the years all the way. As soon as she had placed a delicate high-heeled sandal on the teak deck of the boat, her sharp gaze sweeping over Francesca's natural ash-blonde hair—as opposed to her own, which was clearly the result of an expensive hairdresser—it was

clear from her tight-lipped response to the younger
girl's greeting that the cruise was doomed from the
start. Gloria's remark, on being shown the very large
double cabin and *en-suite* bathroom situated at the
front of the schooner of, 'What a dump! Give me Palm
Beach any time!' seemed to set the tone. It was rapidly
followed by imperious demands for her luggage, the
whereabouts of her stepdaughter's cabin, and a *very*
stiff drink.

'You'd better make that a triple vodka—and go easy
on the tonic,' Gloria rasped, before swiftly inspecting
all the other cabins—just to make absolutely certain
that she had been given the biggest and the best
accommodation on board. 'And I expect lunch to be
served in twenty minutes,' she added curtly, before
retiring to her cabin and slamming the door loudly
behind her.

Busy hauling what seemed to be tons of luggage
down into the saloon, Francesca cursed Matt under her
breath. The Wagners were his friends, right? So, even
if Ben Wagner turned out to be an angel, Matt *must* be
out of his mind to have invited Gloria on to the boat!
However, when she staggered back up on deck for the
next load of cases she discovered the reason behind her
stepbrother's apparent insanity.

Staring, open-mouthed, at the vision in front of her,
Francesca wondered bemusedly why it had never
occurred to her to question Matt's statement about the
Wagners' 'young daughter'. Quite why she had
expected a small girl, she had no idea. But the tall,
long-limbed and voluptuous-looking woman, whom
Matt was oh, so carefully helping up on to the deck,

was certainly no child! However, from the way the awful man was smiling down at the amazingly beautiful, striking redhead, Francesca had no problem in understanding why he was prepared to put up with her stepmother Gloria.

There was no doubt that Lois Wagner was stunning! Draping herself artistically against a mast, while she waited for her luggage to be handed up from the dinghy, the other girl was definitely a sight for sore eyes. Clearly Matt thought so—and who could blame him? Francesca told herself gloomily, trying to suppress a feeling of sheer blind jealousy as she gazed at the vision in front of her.

Her instinctive reaction had *nothing* to do with Matt, she assured herself firmly as he beckoned her forward to help with the extra cases. It was merely envy— which *anyone* could be expected to feel when faced with a girl with such an outstandingly beautiful face and figure.

'Lois—I want you to meet Francesca,' Matt said, putting an arm around his girlfriend's slim waist. 'She's going to be cooking for us, and I'm sure that she will do everything she can to make your trip as comfortable as possible,' he added. Unfortunately, the warmth in his voice was not reflected in the hard green eyes, which carried the unmistakable warning, '*and woe betide you if you don't*!' as he turned to face Francesca.

'Yes, I'll certainly—er—do my best,' she muttered, aware of the redheaded girl's eyes swiftly raking her figure from head to toe. Not that *she* needs to worry about any competition, Francesca thought glumly, wishing she had changed into one of her new outfits. It was clearly a conclusion which had already been arrived at by Lois. Murmuring a polite greeting, she gave the pale English girl's crumpled white shorts and limp T-shirt a pitying glance before gazing down with satisfaction at her own skin-tight white leather mini-skirt over long, deeply tanned legs.

'Goodness, it sure is hot out here in the Caribbean!' Lois exclaimed, giving Matt a lazy smile as she slowly removed the matching white leather jacket, to reveal a sleeveless and very low-cut blue silk vest clinging tightly to her full breasts.

For an impromptu strip-tease, it really was a great performance, Francesca thought sourly. I wonder what she does for an encore? And how on earth did Lois manage to look so fresh and *soignée* after her long flight on the aircraft? Life really was extremely unfair at times!

'Well, hurry up and take Lois's luggage down to her cabin,' Matt's curt voice broke into her thoughts, bringing her sharply down to earth.

'And when you've unpacked my cases I'd just love you to run me a shower,' Lois told her, a thread of steel underlying her softly voiced request. 'And maybe you can fetch me a nice cool drink, too?'

Struggling not to tell the other girl to get lost—why couldn't she unpack her own things, for heaven's sake?—Francesca was aware that Matt was grimly enjoying her discomfiture. Well, if the double-crossing swine thought that she was going to cave in and let him slide out of his part of their bargain, he was very much mistaken. After all, she only had to survive this sort of

nonsense for the next fourteen days, right? Anyone
with an ounce of spirit ought to be able to manage that!

However, only forty-eight hours later Francesca wasn't
nearly so certain about her chances of survival. In fact,
as she leaned back against the large padded cushions,
which she'd placed against the front rail of the boat,
she was sure that if the yacht had possessed a gas oven
she'd have put her head in it long ago.

Brushing the hot, damp curls from her brow, she
almost groaned aloud with pleasure as the fresh, light
currents of air wafted through her long hair. It was her
favourite time of day here in the Caribbean. The cool
early-evening breeze was rustling through the fronds of
the palm trees which fringed the small deserted bay in
which *Silver Lady* was anchored, the only sound to
disturb the tranquil scene being the occasional cries of
the seagulls as they swept by overhead.

Glancing towards the sandy beach, she noted the
faint grey plumes of smoke rising from the charcoal
barbeque, which Calvin had offered to light for her.
With any luck, Francesca told herself wryly, she had at
least an hour of peace and quiet before she had to
begin cooking the steaks for dinner. In the meantime,
it was bliss to be up here—well away from the heat of
the galley and the incessant demands of Gloria and
Lois Wagner on her time—and her patience.

The Wagners! Within an hour of their arrival on the
yacht, Francesca's depressed spirits had hit a new low.
Having to cope with Matt was bad enough. However,
she'd had a terrible presentiment that anything he
might dish out was simply *peanuts* when compared to

the trials, and the tribulations, which clearly lay ahead of her. And she'd been so right! Even allowing for the two women's initial tiredness and feelings of jet lag after their flight from the States, Francesca would have had to be blind, deaf and dumb not to realise that they both spelled trouble with a capital 'T'!

Ben Wagner was, as Matt had said, a really sweet man. With his shock of white hair, and clothed in a pair of old denim shorts, he was clearly in his element on board the boat. He was warm and friendly, happy to muck in and help out in any crisis, and no one would ever have guessed that he was a multi-millionaire many times over. But when it came to his wife Gloria—not to mention his unbelievably awful daughter Lois. . . Francesca simply couldn't imagine why someone hadn't strangled them both years ago!

'Hey—how's it going?' Calvin asked, walking across the deck to adjust some ropes on a nearby mast. 'I see Cinderella has managed to get out of the kitchen for a while!' he laughed.

'*Ssh*. . .for goodness' sake—keep your voice down!' she hissed, grimacing up at him as she placed a warning finger in front of her lips. 'I've just escaped up here for a breath of fresh air and—hopefully!—those awful women don't know where I am,' she added with a grin.

Calvin gave her a beaming smile. 'Hey—no problem! They're still dead to the world, sleeping off all that rum punch they drank at lunchtime!'

'Just as long as they leave me alone for a while, I don't care *what* they do,' Francesca said with feeling, leaning back on the cushions and closing her eyes.

Never in her wildest dreams could she have imagined

that being in charge of the domestic duties of a boat could be *such* an exhausting business. Matt was certainly getting his money's worth out of her, she thought grimly, easing her aching muscles into a more comfortable position. Because it had very quickly become apparent that she wasn't just the cook on this cruise. Oh, no! Not content with making her clean up the damn boat—after his business friends had left it in such a filthy mess—Matt also expected her to fulfil the roles of chief housekeeper, stewardess, and general dogsbody for Gloria and Lois. The loathsome, odious man was obviously a complete and utter *rat*.

However, maybe it was just as well that she'd been so busy over the past two days. It had meant that she and Matt had barely spoken more than a curt word to each other—and then only when it was strictly necessary. If she'd had any time on her hands she might have taken the opportunity to think of some really gruesome, extremely painful ways of terminating his existence. Unfortunately, she was just too tired and weary at the end of each day to do more than retire to her cabin and fall immediately into a deep, exhausted sleep.

Apart from the trauma at the time of her stepmother's early death, Francesca couldn't remember when she had ever felt quite so lonely and miserable. Even reminding herself early this morning that she only had to face twelve more days of purgatory hadn't seemed to help.

In fact, trying to look on the bright side of her present existence was clearly a waste of time, she told herself with a heavy sigh. The only faintly encouraging bit of good news was that she hadn't yet been seasick. Although that could well be due to the fact that, since his guests had come aboard two days ago, Matt had only sailed the yacht very slowly up the east coast of Grenada.

'Puddling around', was what he called it—but it was quite enough for her. She hadn't been joking when she'd told Matt that she was not cut out for a jolly yo-ho-ho life on the ocean wave. Which was just about the only thing she had in common with that ghastly woman Gloria Wagner!

The Wagners' first meal on board had proved to be a total disaster. The lunch itself had started on a sour note. Thanks to the long shower taken by Lois—during which she had clearly washed her long red hair—the fresh-water system had been completely emptied.

'Oh, gee—I'm sorry,' Lois simpered, casting an appealing little-girl-lost glance at Matt from beneath her long black eyelashes.

'Matt doesn't mind—not when you're looking so gorgeous, dear,' Gloria said, casting an approving, complacent glance at her stepdaughter. Since Lois was wearing a skin-tight pair of white trousers and a skimpy jade-green silk vest, which displayed a considerable amount of her large, firm breasts, Francesca could well understand why Matt had genially agreed with her stepmother.

If I'd used up the water—he'd have killed me! Francesca fumed silently to herself, angrily banging a saucepan into the small sink in the galley. She would now have to wait for at least two hours before she could do the washing-up. And anyone who wanted a shower before six o'clock in the evening was going to be way out of luck.

'What on earth is *this*?' Gloria demanded, grimacing down at the plate which Francesca had placed before her. 'It looks kinda weird to me,' the older woman added, suspiciously jabbing the food with her fork.

'It's *ceviche*, and there's a salad and——'

'I didn't ask what it's called,' Gloria snapped. 'What *is* it?' And when Francesca told her, enumerating the various ingredients, Gloria gave a dramatic shriek. '*Raw fish*? You're seriously expecting me to eat *raw* fish?' she demanded, pushing the plate violently away from her.

'But it's delicious, really it is,' Francesca protested. 'The snapper fillets have been marinaded in lime and orange juice, with the chopped-up onions and peppers——'

'Ugh!' Gloria said firmly, before advising her husband and Lois not to eat something that was likely to give them ptomaine poisoning.

'It tastes pretty good to me,' Ben Wagner retorted, tucking happily into his food.

Francesca noted that Matt was also busy clearing his plate, although the swine hadn't said a word on her behalf. However, there seemed nothing she could do to persuade the two women that their lives weren't in danger. They didn't seem to care for her chicken and artichoke casserole, either. The fact that Ben and Matt cheerfully wolfed down their helpings did nothing to improve her sense of deep gloom and foreboding, as she later found herself scraping half the food she'd prepared into the rubbish bin.

Her depression had deepened even further during the next two days. Nothing she could do was right—everything was wrong. Gloria, for instance, clearly couldn't wait until she could get her feet back on dry land. Not bothering to hide the fact, she'd proceeded to take her resentment out on Francesca—the only person she could offend with impunity. And Lois, who had briefly begun to be slightly more friendly, had, under her stepmother's influence, soon reverted to her usual spoilt, demanding character. In fact, her whole life now seemed to be dominated by the never-ending, raucously strident female cries of 'Fran-*ches*-ca. . .', which heralded yet another demand for this or that.

And Matt was absolutely no help at all. Thankfully, she'd had almost no contact with him, although she had noted that he was keeping a harsh, critical eye on the meals she was providing. Luckily, he'd seemed pleased with her efforts—and so he should, she thought grimly. The roast beef *provençal*, which she'd served for dinner last night, had taken ages to prepare, mostly because Lois had, once again, drained the fresh-water tank. However, Francesca had nearly fainted dead away with surprise when Matt had gone so far as to praise the hot crab soufflé, which she'd prepared for lunch today.

All the same, she was still *very* angry with Matt. How could a man—who was supposed to be such a financial wizard—make so many crazy, sweeping judgements about people? He seemed to think the Wagners were great, while appearing to be completely insane as far she herself was concerned. Especially since most of those really disgusting, totally slanderous things he'd said about her the night they'd had dinner on the yacht could so easily be disproved. And it wasn't only her. His quite extraordinary attitude towards her friend Rupert ffinch-Rawlings almost defied belief.

She had no idea how Matt knew that Rupert had recently moved into her flat in London. But so what? Why shouldn't she have him to stay for a few weeks while his own apartment was being completely redecorated? And as for Matt's crazy assumption that Rupert was her 'live-in lover'. . . If it wasn't so stupid she'd scream with laughter. Rupert was a good friend, she enjoyed working with him, and they were both looking forward to owning the art gallery. However, that was the beginning and end of their relationship, since he wasn't at all sexually interested in women. And so she could have told Matt—*if* he'd bothered to ask her, instead of jumping to all those silly wrong conclusions.

A voice calling from one of the cabins down below broke in to her gloomy thoughts. 'Fran-*ches*-ca? Where *is* that stupid girl?'

'Oh, no!' she groaned, sighing heavily as she sat up, brushing a tired hand through her long ash-blonde hair.

'No problem!' Calvin, who was still working on the deck, waved her back as she began to rise. 'I'll go and see what they want.'

'You're an angel!' Francesca breathed thankfully. 'I expect Gloria has lost her electric hair-rollers yet again. And *please* can you try and stop Lois from using up *all* the fresh water?'

'No problem,' Calvin assured her with a grin, before moving quickly away across the deck.

Francesca gave a heavy sigh and sank thankfully

back down on to the cushions. What she would have done without Calvin's help and assistance on this cruise, she had simply no idea. The tall man with his constant cheerful words, 'No problem!' had definitely helped to preserve her sanity. In fact, Calvin—who acted as Matt's right-hand man on the boat, as well as helping to sail *Silver Lady*—had become a really staunch friend.

A faint background buzz of an engine, which had been gradually intruding on the peaceful silence of the bay, seemed to be growing louder. Sitting up and shielding her eyes from the glare of the sun, now low down on the horizon, she saw a small boat approaching the yacht. Even from this distance, Francesca immediately recognised the broad-shouldered figure seated at the helm. It looked as though Matt and Ben Wagner had decided to return earlier than expected from their snorkelling expedition to a nearby island. Which meant, she realised with a heavy sigh, that her brief respite from work was well and truly over.

'That sure was a lot of fun!' Ben called out to her as he climbed up on to the rear deck of the yacht. But although she smiled and gave him a brief wave of greeting, her eyes were irresistibly drawn to the tall, lithe figure of the man following closely behind him.

The breath seemed to catch in her throat, her cheeks growing hot as she saw that Matt was wearing only a pair of brief swimming-trunks above long mahogany-coloured legs which seemed to stretch forever. A shaft of evening sunlight gleamed over his magnificent physique, lending a deep glow to the smooth, deeply tanned skin rippling over the muscles of his arms and broad shoulders, highlighting the dark hair covering his deep chest.

With an abrupt sense of shock and despair, she realised that, despite her strong hostile feelings of anger and resentment against Matt, she was still violently affected by his powerful masculine attraction. There seemed nothing she could do to combat the instinctive, shivering response that suddenly gripped her stomach.

Standing rooted to the deck, stunned and confused by her emotional reaction to a man whom she was quite certain she detested, the spell was broken as she heard another loud cry from below.

'Fran-*ches*-ca. . .?'

Calvin ran up the companion-way from the saloon below, giving her a brief grimace and a helpless shrug of his shoulders. 'They want a cold drink, and the ice machine don't seem to be working.'

'Oh—er—yes, I. . . I'll see what I can do,' she mumbled.

Moving as quickly as she could, she tried to give Matt's practically naked figure a wide berth. It wasn't an easy task. The deck of the elegant ninety-foot long schooner contained not only two large masts, with their furled, bulky sails flapping in the light breeze, but also several wide-open hatches over each of the compartments below. The heavy coils of rope were another hazard, and as she found herself almost tripping over one it was only Matt's quick movement—swiftly catching hold of her arm—which stopped her from falling flat on her face.

'Careful!' he warned, his eyes gleaming with sardonic

amusement as he stared down at the flushed face and trembling figure of the girl who was so clearly trying to avoid him.

Mortified to feel her cheeks reddening at the close proximity of his bare chest, only inches away from her own face, Francesca tried to take a quick step backwards. Unfortunately, Matt didn't seem inclined to let go of her arm.

'What's the hurry?' he drawled, his lips widening into a mocking grin as he pulled her shrinking body closer to his own.

'I. . . I've got to go. Gloria and Lois want a drink,' she murmured desperately, bitterly aware that he was merely amusing himself at her expense. In fact, it was only the presence of the other two men on deck which stopped her from giving Matt's shins a hefty kick.

'That sounds like a good idea. Ben and I could do with a beer,' he said, clearly enjoying her discomfiture.

'You won't get anything—not unless you let me go!' she snapped waspishly.

With a careless shrug, he let go of her arm. She took to her heels, scuttling quickly across the deck towards the companion-way which led down to the saloon, and Francesca gritted her teeth as the sound of his dry, cynical laughter echoed in her ears.

'Where in the hell have you been?' a voice demanded angrily.

It was some moments before her eyes, accustomed to the bright glare of the sun outside, adjusted to the dim light within the large interior space of the saloon. And then she saw Lois, standing in the doorway of her cabin at the far end of the room.

'I can't wear this!' The other girl waved a garment in the air. 'Hasn't anyone ever taught you how to iron a dress?' she added with a sneer.

Taking a deep breath, Francesca mentally counted up to ten before saying quietly, 'I will, of course, iron it again for you. However, since Matt has decided that we're to have a barbecue on the beach tonight, a silk dress doesn't seem to be *exactly* the right thing to wear,' she added smoothly.

The other girl gave her a quick, suspicious glance. But, when Francesca continued to regard her with a blank expression on her face, Lois gave a sigh of exasperation. 'Well, I guess you could be right, at that,' she admitted slowly.

Behind her carefully controlled features, Francesca was thinking that she wished she looked half as gorgeous and striking as this tall, voluptuous girl. With her flaming red hair—and a temper to match!—Lois would have been outstandingly attractive if it weren't for the sulky expression on her lovely face. As she stood there in the doorway, her curvaceous, seductive figure sketchily clothed in a very brief bikini, it was easy to see why Matt was obviously interested in the girl. And Lois was certainly crazy about him! Still, why should she care? It was none of her business, Francesca was telling herself defiantly as the door of the large master suite at the front of the yacht was opened.

'What does one have to do to get a drink on this damn boat?' Gloria Wagner demanded aggressively.

Francesca's heart sank as she gazed at the small, brassy blonde-haired woman. Petite, petulant and poisonous—Francesca had gone to sleep last night while trying to think of some other suitably apt words beginning with 'p'—Gloria was clearly in a *very* bad temper.

'I want a neat vodka, and plenty of ice,' she rasped, placing a trembling hand on her forehead beneath the large white heated hair-rollers. 'Someone should have warned me about those lethal rum punches,' she added, throwing Francesca a vicious look as if it were the English girl's fault that she had a heavy hangover.

'I feel a bit rough, too,' Lois admitted. 'I guess I'll just have some mineral water—with lots of ice.'

Francesca tried not to show her dismay. Calvin had said the ice machine wasn't working. In fact, it had been acting up in a thoroughly temperamental way ever since the Wagners had come aboard. Just one more thing for Gloria to complain about, she thought wearily before telling the two women that she'd get them their drinks as soon as possible.

'See that you do. God—I hate this damn boat!' Gloria snapped, going back into her cabin and slamming the door loudly behind her—an action closely followed by Lois.

In the galley, staring glumly at the ice machine— which was obstinately refusing to work properly— Francesca wondered, not for the first time, whether she wasn't having to pay too high a price for the London art gallery. She wouldn't wish Gloria and Lois on her worst enemy! And it really wasn't her fault that she couldn't seem to get on with the other two women. She had tried to be friendly, but had simply given up in the face of their quite extraordinary antagonism.

During the brief period when Lois had been acting

in a slightly more friendly way towards her, she'd told Francesca that she was the daughter of Ben and his first wife, who had died when the girl was a teenager. Since Ben clearly adored his daughter—although he had, unfortunately, spoilt her rotten—it wouldn't have been surprising if the girl had resented her new step-mother, Gloria. However, somewhat surprisingly, they seemed to get on like a house on fire. Maybe because they were so alike, Francesca thought glumly, irritably banging the ice machine with her clenched fist. She hadn't been surprised to learn that Lois had been a very successful model. But, on the other hand, nor had she been surprised when the other girl had added, 'But I gave it up, honey. It was all so boring.' Which may well have been true, but Francesca suspected that Lois hadn't been able to maintain the strict self-discipline required by that exacting profession.

However, there was one thing about which she had no doubts: Lois was clearly anxious to become Mrs Matt Sinclair. And, from the way he was flirting with the girl—not to mention putting his arm around her at every conceivable opportunity!—it looked as though Lois was the girl to whom Matt had said he was expecting to get engaged. And good luck to him! Francesca thought grimly. Because she'd never met a more bad-tempered, spoilt and sulky girl in all her life.

Gritting her teeth and swearing violently under her breath, Francesca gave the machine another hefty thump. 'Come on, you brute—can't you give me more than one lump of ice every twenty minutes?' she was snarling in acute frustration when she nearly jumped out of her skin with shock as a hard, firm hand suddenly gripped her shoulder.

'It's supposed to be the first sign of madness when you start talking to yourself,' a voice drawled sardonically in her ear. Ignoring her startled gasp, Matt placed a hand on her other shoulder. 'But if you've gone so far out of sight that you're now holding conversations with machinery. . .well—I guess there's no hope for you!'

Francesca's lips tightened with annoyance as his low, sensual laugh seemed to echo around the small galley. It was absolutely maddening the way he always seemed to catch her off guard—and apparently making an utter fool of herself.

'I can't get this stupid machine to work,' she ground out angrily.

'Maybe if you tried cleaning it out and changing the filter you might have some success,' he pointed out in an irritatingly bland tone of voice.

'Nobody has ever said anything about having to regularly clean out that machine,' she grumbled, before realising that Matt's hands were still on her shoulders— and that she was effectively trapped by the strong, muscular body standing so closely behind her. 'Why— er—why didn't you tell me about the. . .the filter, and having to clean it? she demanded breathlessly, then quickly turned around and tried to push him away.

And then she discovered that she had just made a grave mistake.

The heat of his skin seemed to be scorching the palms of her hands, her fingers trembling amid the dark curly hair on his bare chest as she stared bemusedly up in to his face.

'What. . .what are you doing in here?' she demanded huskily.

'What am *I* doing in here?' he echoed, raising a dark cynical eyebrow as he stared down at her silently for a moment. 'How extraordinary!' he added with a grim smile, his fingers tightening menacingly on her slim shoulders. 'I was under the impression that I owned this yacht—but maybe you know better?'

CHAPTER SIX

FRANCESCA stared glumly up at the tall, broad-shouldered figure looming over her.

Matt was quite correct, of course. It *was* his boat, and it had been stupid of her to question his presence in the galley. But there was no need for him to have crept up on her like that. And he *definitely* shouldn't be walking around this yacht wearing nothing but that shockingly brief towel about his slim hips, she thought distractedly, trying to tear her eyes away from the sight of so much bare tanned flesh.

She'd been horrified to discover—when they'd left the anchorage at Prickly Bay and it was far too late to do anything about it—that Matt was sleeping in the cabin next to hers, at the rear of the schooner. Not that she'd heard anything from him, of course, other than the occasional sounds of a drawer being opened, or a cupboard door being slammed shut. All the same. . .

Francesca knew that she was probably being ridiculously apprehensive. However, she was finding it very disturbing, when she fell exhausted into bed each night, to know that he was lying just the other side of the flimsy wooden partition. And, even though she'd taken every precaution when using the small bathroom—which they had to share with each other—she couldn't expect to avoid him forever.

'No water?'

'What. . .?' She raised her head, gazing up at him in confusion.

Matt gave an exasperated sigh. 'I want to know *why* I can't have a shower. What's happened to all the water?'

She closed her eyes for a moment, trying to ignore the tanned male chest only inches away from her face. Unfortunately, unless she stopped breathing, it was proving impossible not to absorb the musky masculine scent of his cologne mingling with the aroma of his own warm skin. Taking a deep breath, she made a determined effort to pull herself together.

'If. . .um. . .if there isn't any fresh water it's nothing to do with me,' she muttered huskily, staring fixedly at a spot well to the right of his tall figure.

'I thought I told you, and Calvin, to run the engine for two hours—while Ben and I were snorkelling?' he queried coldly.

'Yes, but——'

'And I distinctly remember explaining to you—more than once!—that the main purpose of the exercise was to run the desalination outfit, as well as charging the batteries.'

She bristled, feeling her cheeks flushing at the sharp, caustic sting in his voice.

'Yes, you gave us your orders,' she snapped, quickly turning her head to glare up at him with stormy blue eyes. 'And, yes, Calvin and I were all set to carry them out.'

'So—why didn't you?' he demanded brusquely.

Her face burned as she struggled to keep her temper.

'Let's take it from the top, shall we?' she said through clenched teeth. 'When you run the engine, it makes a lot of noise, right?'

'Correct,' he snapped.

'OK. So when Calvin obeyed your orders and switched it on—your girlfriend and her stupid stepmother promptly had a bad case of hysterics. And, if you want to know *why* they were insisting on total silence, it's because Lois and Gloria have spent the whole afternoon fast asleep in their cabins. If you want to know the truth,' she paused, before adding scathingly, 'it was the result of pouring all those strong rum punches down their throats at lunchtime. So if you're going to have a row with anyone. . .' her voice dripped with acid '. . .why don't you have it with them?'

'Don't take that tone of voice with *me!*' he growled angrily, his fingers biting like talons into her shoulders.

'Well—stop ordering me about like a skivvy. . .' she gasped, wincing at the pain he was inflicting on her soft flesh. 'And. . .and take your hands off me—*you foul bully!*'

Blind fury at the sheer injustice of the situation in which she now found herself gave Francesca a strength she didn't know she possessed. Violently twisting herself away from his tight grip, she ducked out from beneath his tall figure, quickly running to the other side of the galley.

Matt spun around to face her. 'You seem to have forgotten that I've bought your services for the next two weeks. . .'

'Correction!' she snapped quickly. 'It's only twelve more days—*thank God*!'

'So if I—or anyone else—give you an order,' he continued harshly, completely ignoring her interjection, 'I expect it to be carried out—*immediately*!'

'Well, you can just take a running jump into the sea!' she retorted defiantly. 'I. . . I'm sick and tired of being shouted at by everyone on this yacht! As far as I'm concerned—those two awful women should have been shot at birth!'

He toook a threatening step forward, his face and eyes as hard as nails. 'I won't have you talking about my guests like that. It's about time I taught you a few manners!' he hissed with soft, blood-curdling menace.

'Oh, yes—you and who else?' she jeered, her temper by now well out of control. And then, as he began moving purposefully towards her, she quickly decided not to push her luck any further. One swift glance at the grim expression on his face was enough to send her dashing, as fast as her legs could carry her, out of the galley and towards the sanctuary of her cabin.

Slamming the door behind her, and breathlessly leaning back against it as she strove to calm down, Francesca tried to think what she was going to do next. She couldn't hide in here forever, of course. Especially as she was going to have to see to the barbeque.

At the thought of having to provide yet another gargantuan meal, Francesca gave a heavy sigh. Maybe it was the sea air, but everyone on the boat seemed to have the most amazing appetites. Even thin, scraggy Gloria, who was given to quoting the late Duchess of Windsor—'No woman can be too rich or too thin'—

managed to eat an astonishing amount of food. And as for Lois—how *did* that girl keep her magnificent figure when she was always raiding the icebox for her favourite chocolate ice-cream. . .?

Her thoughts were interrupted by the sound of a drawer, or a cupboard, being noisily slammed shut in the adjacent cabin. And a moment later a fist banged on the door behind her.

'Francesca!' Matt's deep voice sounded heavy with menace. 'Come out of there. I want to talk to you.'

'Go away!' she shouted back.

'Open this door—*at once!*'

'Get lost!' she yelled, knowing that she was quite safe for the moment. Matt might be a hateful man— but at least he wasn't the type to go around breaking down doors.

A brief second later she discovered that she had— unfortunately—not only made a grave mistake. . .but that she was also, apparently, a *very* bad judge of character.

Matt's simple answer to her defiance was to lift his foot and drive it hard up against the flimsy wooden door. His violent action resulted in her being swiftly catapulted across the small room to land sprawling on the bed, winded and gasping for breath.

'How. . .how dare you. . .?' she panted, angrily brushing the swirling cloud of long ash-blonde hair from her brow as she tried to sit up.

'How dare *you* talk about my guests in such a derogatory fashion?' he retorted grimly, his face seemingly carved from granite as he stared across at her, his mouth set in a hard, uncompromising line. 'You're nothing but the hired help around here—and don't you forget it!'

'Well. . .the "hired help" has just resigned!' she retorted breathlessly, her heart thudding like a sledge-hammer at the menace projected by Matt's tall, dominating figure.

'Oh, yes. . .?' he drawled ominously, turning to kick the door shut before slamming across the small brass bolt, which she had stupidly forgotten to close when she'd run into the room.

'Yes! I've had enough of you—*and* your guests!' she threw at him, furiously struggling to free herself from the loose bedsheet, which seemed to have become entangled with her limbs. 'I'm getting off this boat at the next port of call. And there's nothing you can do about it!'

He leaned casually back against the door. 'I can stop you getting the art gallery you've set your heart on—or had you forgotten about that little item?' he purred dangerously, his lips curving into a sardonic smile at her continuing efforts to try and extricate herself from the bedclothes.

'Do what you like—you. . .you rotten blackmailer! See if I care!'

Francesca knew that she sounded childish—and that it was foolish to continue to defy him, but she seemed to be in the grip of a strange force that was almost compelling her to do so. Of course she'd care about losing the art gallery. But she was rapidly coming to the conclusion that the price he was demanding was far too high. And not just in having to put up with Gloria and Lois. It was Matt himself who was increasingly becoming a far greater threat to her peace of mind than either of those two awful women.

Finally managing to throw aside the sheet, she belatedly noticed that he must have used those few minutes—before charging into her cabin—to put on a pair of faded blue denim shorts. Clinging tightly to his slim hips and powerful, muscular thighs, they were *not* an improvement on that disgracefully small towel he'd been wearing. Why couldn't the man clothe himself in something more. . .well, something more suitable? He ought to be ashamed of being seen in anything *quite* so outrageously sexy! Her cheeks grew hot as she realised the direction her confused thoughts were taking.

'And I'm not having a half-baked mutiny on *my* ship!' Matt was saying harshly, as she made a determined effort to ignore his strong masculine appeal.

'Well, that's just too bad,' she muttered, finally managing to sit up on the bed—a task made harder by the soft, springy mattress and the gentle sway of the boat, 'because I'm not taking any more from those two damn prima donnas!' she added firmly.

'Keep your voice down!' he growled, casting a quick glance at the open hatch above them. 'There's no need to tell everyone on deck all about your trifling complaints.'

'*Trifling*. . .?' she cried, ignoring his terse warning. 'Even if you paid me a thousand dollars a day to look after them—it *still* wouldn't be enough,' she told him bitterly. '"Come here. . .go there. . ." I don't seem to have a moment's peace and quiet. It's a complete miracle that I ever manage to produce a meal on time!'

'Have you quite finished?' he enquired coldly.

'No—I certainly haven't!' she snarled, quickly standing up as she finally managed to place her feet on the floor.

'You've got *no* idea what it's like trying to cope with them,' she continued angrily. 'Every time your girlfriend announces that she's going to wash her hair I have to dash off and fill all the saucepans as quickly as I can—because that's the end of any fresh water for at least two hours. And you can bet your bottom dollar that *immediately* Lois has drained the tank—*dear* Gloria will start shouting because she hasn't got any cold water to drink!'

'I'm not interested in——'

'Yes—I *know* you're not "interested",' she raged. 'The great Matt Sinclair is far too busy giving the orders around here to bother himself about how they're supposed to be carried out!' she added stormily, her temper by now well out of control. 'Well, when you marry Lois you'd better make sure that you've got a *really* good supply of water at hand. Because, when she decides to wash her hair, I can *guarantee* that she's going to drain a thousand-gallon tank—in five seconds flat!'

Francesca's temper was not improved as she saw his broad shoulders shaking with amusement.

'Well, well. . .!' he murmured, walking slowly towards her. 'It doesn't sound as though you like Lois very much, hmm?'

'That—er—that isn't the point. . .' She gulped nervously, restrained by the edge of the bed from being able to back away from his advancing figure. 'Although I suppose Lois isn't *quite* as bad as ghastly Gloria. But

you do seem to be getting the message—at last!' she
added with heavy sarcasm.

'Oh, yes, I'm getting the message, all right.' He gave
a low, sensual laugh which sent her heart thumping in
a crazy uneven rhythm. 'You're obviously green with
jealousy.'

'*Me*? Jealous of Lois. . .?' Francesca gave a brittle
shriek of laughter, which even in her own ears sounded
far too false and edgy. 'Why on earth should I be
jealous? I'm sure you two *wonderful* people fully
deserve each other,' she ground out furiously as he
came to a halt in front of her trembling figure.

'So—you approve of my marriage to Lois, do you?'
he drawled softly.

Matt didn't move as he stared silently down at her.
But all at once the atmosphere in the small, confined
cabin seemed to become highly charged with an unmistakable sexual tension. The fury and anger seemed to
drain from her body, her mouth becoming suddenly
dry and the blood pounding in her veins as she was
swept by an overpowering, totally crazy urge to throw
herself into his arms. A mad impulse which she swiftly
and ruthlessly crushed without mercy.

'I really couldn't care less who you marry,' she said
as firmly as she could.

'Really. . .?' he murmured.

'Yes, really,' she retorted flatly, ignoring the heavy
scepticism in his voice. 'So why don't you go and
entertain your girlfriend in the saloon? I'm sure she'll
be glad to see you—and maybe you can magic up some
ice from somewhere,' Francesca added, marvelling at
the fact that her voice was managing to sound so cool

and steady as she tried to edge past him towards the door.

'Oh, no—you're not going to escape me that easily!'

His rapid movement gave her no time to escape. With what seemed the speed of light, she found herself imprisoned within his arms, her breasts crushed against his hard bare chest.

Instinctively she jerked violently away from him, the force of her action sending them both sprawling sideways, down on to the bed. While she lay dazed from her involuntary action and its consequences, Matt seemed to have no such problem. Swiftly rolling over to grab her wrists, he forced them back over her head, pinning her to the soft mattress.

'Let me go!' she cried.

'Not until you agree to remain on this yacht,' he drawled, staring down into her stormy blue eyes. 'You're going to keep to the contract you signed—right?'

'Wrong!' she panted breathlessly.

'I think you're making a great mistake,' he mocked softly, quickly moving to cover her slim frame with his body.

'Get away from me!' she screeched, finding herself hopelessly trapped by the heavy weight of the figure lying across her own. She was desperately twisting to try and free herself when she realised, from the darkening gleam in his glinting green eyes and the sudden hardening of the thighs pressing her so closely to the bed, that her struggling body was exciting him.

'There's no need to hurry with your answer,' he murmured, his deep voice as smokily seductive as the hand which was now moving slowly down over the soft flesh of her arm to encircle her full breast.

'No!' she gasped huskily as his fingers brushed tantalisingly over the swollen peak, her heart starting to beat with a slow, heavily choking thud.

It was no good continuing to try and defy him, she realised with dismay. There was no way she could escape—and she was now beginning to feel frightened by the way her body was trembling in primitive response to his touch.

'OK—OK, I give in,' she gulped breathlessly. 'I. . . I'll keep to your damned contract. Now, please. . .please let me go,' she begged.

'Why should I? Maybe I prefer to—er—entertain a girlfriend in here,' he drawled with soft menace.

'I'm not your girlfriend,' she spat angrily, making a last-ditch attempt to wriggle out from beneath him. It achieved nothing, as he clasped her head more firmly, winding his fingers through her long hair.

'I could be persuaded to change my mind,' he breathed thickly.

'I thought you said that. . .that you wouldn't dream of sullying yourself with second-hand goods. . .' she accused him bitterly, recalling his cruel words on her first night in Grenada.

'So I did,' he murmured, his fingers tightening to hold her head firmly imprisoned beneath him. 'And yet—even though I know what you are—I still find you very. . .very desirable.'

'Well, I don't want or desire you. Save your "entertainment" for Lois. I. . . I'm simply not interested!' she gasped, knowing that she was lying through her teeth as her quivering figure was filled with a familiar sick excitement.

She couldn't seem to tear her eyes away from his mouth, swept by a deep longing to feel the hard, sensual lips pressed closely to her own. Her heart was beating so fast that her ears seemed to be filled with its drumming. Oh, lord—what was happening to her?

'Please. . .please let me go,' she pleaded huskily.

'No chance!' he breathed thickly, his eyes growing cloudy beneath their heavy lids as he lowered his dark head towards her.

'I . . . I hate you!' she exclaimed helplessly.

'Oh, darling Francesca! What a rotten little liar you are!' He gave a husky bark of laughter as he buried his face in her fragrant cloud of blonde hair.

He was right, she acknowledged with despair. Every nerve-end in her body seemed to be tingling with excitement, evoking a response it was impossible to resist as his mouth trailed down over her flushed cheeks to brush and tantalise her trembling lips.

A deep knot of tremulous desire flared into pulsating life as she found herself responding blindly and urgently to the sensations engendered by the touch of his warm mouth, moving softly and sensually over her own. Her arms slid up about his neck, her lips parting involuntarily under the delicate pressure, allowing him to slowly and erotically savour the soft moistness within.

Matt's husky murmur of satisfaction at her action did nothing to help her resistance. She seemed powerless to prevent herself from welcoming the demanding possession of his deepening kiss, the potent urgency of the hard male figure pinning her to the mattress. Her breathless pleas for him to stop became inaudible moans beneath the melting sweetness, the soft seduction of his lips.

A shudder shook his tall frame, a deep groan breaking from his throat at the innocent provocation of her body, now moving sensually beneath him as she blindly responded to his increasing ardour.

Since they were totally absorbed by the white-hot heat of their mutual desire, it was some moments before they became aware of an approaching danger.

'Fran-*ches*-ca. . .? Where *is* that damn girl? Fran-*ches*-ca. . .?'

Frozen into momentary paralysis by the sound of Gloria's loud, strident voice in the passageway outside the cabin, Francesca could feel the blood draining from her face and body. Shocked and confused, she was aware of Matt releasing her, swearing violently under his breath as he rolled away across the bed. but it wasn't until the urgency of his low, hissed warning, 'For God's sake—move it!' penetrated the mists in her dazed mind that she realised they were only a hair's breadth away from a disastrous confrontation.

A quick mental picture of Gloria—foaming at the mouth on finding Lois's future husband in *such* a compromising situation—was enough to send Francesca scrambling quickly off the bed. Desperately trying to control the weak trembling in her legs, and frantically tucking her blouse back into her shorts, she rushed blindly towards the door. Unfortunately, she had hardly taken more than a few steps across the small cabin, when she cannoned into Matt's tall, broad-shouldered figure and—once again—she found herself tumbling backwards down on to the bed.

'Fran-*ches*-ca. . .? I know you're hiding in there,' Gloria's voice rasped venomously as she banged on the door. 'Let me in—*at once*!'

It was just like being in the middle of a French farce, Francesca thought, almost choking on a bubble of hysterical laughter as she tried to drag herself off the soft, springy mattress. It was only the sound of a fist beating imperiously on the door, and the sight of Matt's furious expression as he roughly hauled her to her feet, that brought her back to earth with a bump.

Following a swift glance at her clearly overwrought, shaking figure, Matt quickly decided to take matters into his own hands. 'If you make a noise—I'll kill you!' he whispered savagely in her ear, before pushing her roughly into a corner of the small room.

'Francesca—what's going on?' Gloria was demanding as the bolt was drawn back. 'Well—er—well. . .hi there!' the older woman exclaimed as the door opened a few inches to disclose Matt's tall figure.

Holding her breath, and hidden from sight in the small space behind the door where he had so roughly pushed her a moment before, Francesca couldn't see what was going on. But there was no mistaking the bewilderment in Gloria's voice.

'I thought. . .well, I mean. . .isn't this Francesca's cabin? I really could have sworn. . .' Her voice trailed away.

'No,' Matt said firmly. 'I'm afraid you're mistaken, Gloria. Francesca's room is next door.'

'Are you sure?' the older woman queried sharply, before giving a slightly embarrassed laugh. 'Of course, I'm sure it really *is* your cabin, Matt. Only it does seem strange. You see, I just happened to be in here yesterday, because I was. . .um. . .looking for a book I'd lent the girl, and. . .'

'We changed rooms late last night,' he told her in a flat, bored tone of voice. 'Francesca claimed the noise of the anchor being raised and lowered was keeping her awake.'

What an amazing tissue of lies! Francesca told herself, reluctantly admiring Matt's extraordinary power of total invention. If I didn't know better I'd believe him myself! I bet he's had plenty of practice at this sort of bedroom farce, she thought grimly as she felt Gloria give the door a nudge in an effort to see more clearly into the room.

But Matt's superior strength was clearly more than a match for the older woman. 'Did you want anything in particular?' he queried blandly, easily holding the door close to his tall figure, and continuing to impede Gloria's view.

'No, dear, nothing very important.' Gloria's voice sounded as sugary as syrup. 'It was just that Lois and I asked for a drink well over an hour ago. And—well, I don't want to say anything unkind about dear Francesca. . .'

Oh, no? That'll be the day! The younger woman scowled at her through the wooden partition.

'. . .but she's really pretty hopeless, isn't she?' Gloria gave a breathless, tinkling laugh. 'I'm sure she doesn't *mean* to be so rude, or so unhelpful. . .even though dear Lois has tried *so* hard to be friendly. But I'd be grateful if you could have a quiet word with the girl. A little reminder that we *are* your guests, hmm? It would be sad if Ben had to cut short his vacation on this yacht because of a little unpleasantness—wouldn't it?' she queried sweetly.

'Yes, I'll certainly—er—have a word with her,' Matt agreed smoothly.

'Dear Matt—I just *knew* you'd see things my way,' Gloria purred, before turning on her heels and walking slowly away.

Francesca waited, holding her breath, until the sound of Gloria's footsteps had faded into the distance. And then, as Matt closed the door, she sagged with relief against the wall.

'What a really poisonous, vicious woman!' she told him furiously. 'All that business about "I just happened to be in here" is a load of baloney! She was just snooping! Not only has Gloria *never* lent me a book— I very much doubt whether she's ever read one!' Francesca added through gritted teeth.

'You'd better keep your voice down,' Matt told her coolly. 'Knowing Gloria, I expect she's zipped up on deck, and has her ear pressed to that open hatch up there right this minute.'

'Since you clearly know *just* how awful the woman is, why on earth do you put up with her?'

'For Ben's sake, of course,' he drawled.

'*And* for dear Lois's sake—no doubt!' she grated harshly, before she was suddenly swept by a deep wave of embarrassment and shame.

How *could* she have allowed herself to somehow

become 'the other woman'? To have responded so passionately towards Matt, despite having learned that he was intending to marry Lois? She felt sick with humiliation—and the mortification of knowing that after her willing surrender just now he was bound to assume that she was his—simply for the taking!

'Ah, yes—I mustn't forget Lois.' Matt smiled sardonically at the furiously heated, resentful expression on her face before moving across the cabin to open a cupboard door.

'That's *hardly* likely!' Francesca ground out scathingly. She was just about to tell him exactly what she thought about a man who was so clearly a two-timing rat of the first order, when she saw that he was removing her clothes from the cupboard, and throwing them on to the bed. 'Hey—what do you think you're doing?' she demanded angrily.

'I may have been stretching the truth, about our deciding to change rooms, but——'

'*Stretching the truth*. . .?' She gave a short bark of incredulous, caustic laughter. 'Who are you kidding? You were lying your head off!'

Matt grinned. 'Yes, I'm afraid I was! However, we now haven't any choice—we've got to change cabins.' He shrugged. 'I know it's a nuisance, but it's all in a good cause.'

'Your cause—not mine!' she snapped, her blue eyes sparkling with rage as he finished emptying the cupboard, and began transferring his attention to the small, built-in chest of drawers. 'And why I was such an idiot—helping you to save your bacon just now—

I'll never know! Frankly, Matt, you're nothing but a double-crossing, two-timing, arrogant womaniser!'

Infuriatingly, he ignored her outburst, only murmuring ironically, 'I love you too, sweetheart!' as he pulled out a drawer, tossing a pile of frothy underwear on to the bed.

'I *certainly* don't love you!' she hissed through clenched teeth. 'And will you kindly leave my clothes alone?'

'Hmm. . .very nice,' he drawled, holding up a minuscule pair of ivory silk and lace panties and matching bra, which she'd bought in St George's. 'These look expensive.'

'Since you paid for them, I'm happy to tell you that they were *very* expensive!' she retorted, blushing furiously as she quickly snatched them from his hands.

Matt gave her a slow, cynical smile. 'In which case I look forward to seeing you in those ridiculous garments—and to removing them, of course!' he added with a low, husky laugh.

'No way!' she blazed, incensed at the sheer arrogance of the man. 'If you so much as lay one finger on me, I'll. . . I'll. . .'

He raised a dark, sardonic eyebrow, an expression of lazy amusement on his face as she hesitated for a moment. 'You'll do—what?' he mocked.

'OK—I didn't want to make this threat, because I happen to think that it's a pretty nasty thing to do to another woman,' she told him breathlessly. 'But, if you force your attentions on me, I. . . I'll tell Lois *exactly* what was going on before Gloria interrupted us just now.'

'"Force my attentions"?' he laughed. 'For a girl with your track record, don't you think that sounds just a little bit old-fashioned?' he taunted.

The sudden hard, intent glint in his eyes played havoc with her nervous system, and she found herself trembling as he began moving slowly towards her.

'I suppose it's useless to keep telling you that I haven't a track record—of any kind?' she muttered.

'You're right—it is. However, you are also quite right. . .telling tales would be a nasty thing to do—and not for the reasons you might suppose,' he told her with cold, silky menace. 'I'm not worried about Lois— because she simply wouldn't believe that you're a threat to her,' he added with brutal frankness. 'But it would be the perfect excuse, which Gloria is just looking for, to get Ben off this yacht.'

'I. . . I don't know what you mean,' Francesca muttered, her eyes shifting warily beneath his fierce gaze as she found herself backed up against the wall.

'Didn't you hear Gloria's final parting shot?' he grated. 'She's quite capable of making good the threat—to stop her husband's vacation before it's even started. And I'm sufficiently fond of Ben to make sure that doesn't happen,' he added grimly.

The hard, determined note in his voice as he leaned forward sent shivers of fear running down her spine. It was a warning—if she had needed any such reminder— of the folly in defying this seemingly invincible man.

Calling on all her reserves of strength, she took a deep breath. 'I agree that Ben's a nice man, and no—I don't want to spoil his holiday. But I meant what I said. If you touch me, ever again,' she added shakily,

'I'm going to tell everyone the truth—and to hell with the consequences!'

His icy green eyes bored down into hers for a long moment. 'Not touch you? Like this. . .?' he murmured softly, raising a hand to the pulse thudding nervously in her throat. 'Or like this. . .' he added in a whisper as his fingers slid slowly down over her breast, the nipple hardening beneath his expert touch.

'Don't!' Francesca moaned, helplessly trying to thrust him away. 'Why can't you leave me alone?'

'I don't know why,' he told her flatly, his face hardening into a steel mask. 'Maybe it's a grim joke on the part of fate. Or maybe it's just nemesis.' He shrugged. 'I only know that, after having arranged and schemed to get you on this yacht, I now find myself caught fast—enmeshed in the very same web I had woven to catch you.'

'I don't understand what you're talking about,' she wailed. 'What about Lois?'

'As far as you and I are concerned—Lois is totally irrelevant!' he drawled coldly.

'How can you be so. . .so cold-blooded and ruthless?' Francesca cried. She actively disliked Lois, but she couldn't help being appalled at his cavalier attitude towards the other girl.

He stared at her silently for a moment, before raising a hand to gently tuck a stray coil of hair behind her ear. His lips twisted into a bitter smile as she flinched and trembled at the feel of his fingers on her skin.

'It's very simple,' he said quietly. 'I want you—and I've had to face the fact that I *must* have you. That's all there is to it.'

'You're crazy!' she whispered, suddenly feeling badly frightened by the flat, hard note of certainty in his deep voice. 'I. . . I meant what I said. I don't want——'

'Oh, but you do!' Matt gave a harsh bark of cruel laughter before turning to stride across the cabin towards the door. 'You go up in flames every time I touch you. Believe me, *darling*,' he taunted, 'I've had a lot of experience with women, and your body is telling me the truth—even if you aren't capable of doing so!'

And then he was gone, only the sound of his sardonic laughter echoing faintly behind him as he ran up the rear companion-way on to the deck.

CHAPTER SEVEN

IT WAS an almost unbearably hot, sticky night. To Francesca, tossing and turning as she stared wide-eyed up through the open hatch in her cabin at the stars twinkling in the dark sky above, it appeared to be endless. As she desperately tried to seek oblivion in sleep there seemed nothing she could do to prevent Matt's cruel, taunting words from running like an evil refrain through her tired mind.

After their disastrous confrontation, she'd barely had any time to compose herself before the sheer necessity of feeding those on board the yacht had forced her into the galley. Having to keep a watchful eye on the steaks cooking over the hot charcoal, she had successfully managed to keep well away from Matt during the barbeque. But she'd been acutely conscious of his hard green eyes flicking dangerously over her nervous, trembling figure throughout the evening.

To add to her problems. . .it had soon become apparent that Gloria—even more aggressively demanding than usual—hadn't been entirely convinced by Matt's glib explanation about the reason why he and Francesca had switched cabins. It was also clear that she had passed her suspicions on to Lois. After trying to take no notice of the two other women's bitchy, pointed remarks, which Matt—the swine!—had blandly ignored, Francesca had been in a state of severe nervous tension.

However, when it came to Lois—pettishly demanding to know just *when* she was intending to return to England—Francesca could only reply with a brief snort of grim, hollow laughter. It would have been a pleasure to tell Lois the truth: that, given even *half* a chance, she'd have happily jumped on the next plane to London! Unfortunately, the other girl wouldn't have believed her. . .or the fact that Matt clearly had no intention of allowing her to escape his clutches.

Although it was such a hot and humid night, Francesca could feel herself burning as she recalled the humiliating ease with which Matt had firmly squashed her threat of resignation. Her cheeks flushed in the darkness at the memory of her pathetic lack of resistance when she'd found herself in his arms. Even more mortifying had been her frenzied, uninhibited response; the spineless way in which she had so quickly succumbed to the force and power of Matt's practised lovemaking. All these hours later, her body was still throbbing with unfulfilled desire, her senses clamouring for release from the excitement engendered by his devastating kiss.

Tossing and turning restlessly throughout the night, tormented by the memory of her own weakness, she finally forced herself to recognise the truth: she—who had been so certain, so confident, that, after eight years, Matt's strong physical attraction no longer had the power to excite or disturb her—had been betrayed by her own emotions. Despite everything that had happened in the past—and despite the intervening years—nothing, it seemed, could change the feelings she still had for the man who had misjudged her so cruelly. And Matt was *still* continuing to view her as if through the wrong end of a telescope, she reminded herself miserably.

However, it was almost a relief to admit the truth to herself at last. She'd fought tooth and nail against acknowledging the fact, but this fiery ecstasy and despair, this burning, passionate desire scorching through her trembling limbs could be nothing else but love. Matt had been right. She *did* go up in flames whenever she was near him. And yes. . .she *did* want him—now and for always. But, if she was prepared to acknowledge the truth about her own emotions, she had no illusions about his. Matt might want her—he had even, with chilling determination, said that he *must* have her—but he'd only been speaking in a purely sexual context. His reference to his experience with other women had, unfortunately, made that quite clear. As far as she could see, the verb 'to love' didn't seem to form part of his vocabulary; Matt might have decided to marry Lois, but it was obvious that he didn't love her either.

Francesca felt totally exhausted by the traumatic events of the day, and yet the blessed relief of sleep continued to evade her. She couldn't seem to prevent herself from thinking about Matt and Lois, her imagination running riot with tortuous images of their two naked figures closely entwined. Was he, in fact, making love to the other girl in her cabin right this very minute?

Racked with pain and jealousy, she rolled over to

bury her head in the pillows, her slender body shaken by deep sobs of bitter, wretched misery and desolation.

Francesca woke up the next morning feeling terrible—tired and morose; her depression wasn't helped by a headache, which began throbbing as soon as she lifted her head from the pillow. However, after squinting down at her watch and seeing that it was a few minutes past seven o'clock, she knew it was no good thinking that she could lie here for even a little longer. Not only would Gloria go up the wall if she didn't get her usual huge breakfast, but the dreaded ice machine was still waiting to be taken apart and cleaned.

Flinching at the pain in her head, she swung her legs off the bed, dragging herself over to the chest of drawers. It had been a thorough nuisance to have to change cabins—just one more black mark to set down against Matt, she thought grimly. However, by the time she'd showered, taken some aspirins and put on another of the outfits she'd bought in St George's—a pair of pale blue, light cotton shorts and a matching sleeveless T-shirt—Francesca was beginning to feel marginally better.

Dragging a brush through her long, tangled hair, she studied her image in the mirror. Where, she wondered, was the girl who had arrived in Grenada with such high hopes? Was it possible that this tired-looking creature, gazing so wearily back at her, was one and the same person? Only a few days ago she'd felt full of life and confidence, excitedly looking forward to owning her own art gallery in Bond Street. Now, staring at the red-rimmed eyes and the distraught, nervously apprehensive expression on the girl's pale face, she totally failed to recognise herself.

What a truly awful, disastrous can of worms this trip to the Caribbean was turning out to be. How *could* she be so foolish as to be still in love with Matt? It was a question which she had asked herself incredulously throughout the long, hot night. And even now, as the sun began to rise up well over the horizon, she still hadn't found an answer.

At least during the run-up to breakfast she could be sure of some peace and quiet, she thought gratefully, walking through into the galley and tying an apron around her slim waist. And, she reasoned while struggling to mend the ice machine, having to be active must surely be better than lying down in her cabin feeling sorry for herself. In fact, she *must* stop being so spineless. That Matt could never reciprocate her love might well seem the end of the world to her—and, oh, yes, *it did*!—but common sense said that of course it wasn't. Given time, she was bound to get over him. . . Well, she'd simply *have to*, wouldn't she? she told herself, savagely beating the batter for Ben's pancakes.

As the aspirins began to take effect and the pounding ache in her head slowly began to subside, Francesca found herself able to think more clearly about her dire situation. Try as she might, she could think of no avenue of escape from Matt—certainly not until the end of this cruise. Even wild schemes, such as jumping ashore at the first opportunity, failed to stand up to more than a moment's contemplation. Matt had taken her passport—goodness knows where he'd put it—and so, even if she managed to get off the boat and make her way to one of the small island airports, she still wouldn't be able to leave the Caribbean.

It was an impasse to which she still hadn't found the answer by the time that the others on the yacht were assembling in the saloon for breakfast. In fact, the only firm resolution she'd come up with was that, as far as Matt was concerned, she *must* appear totally cool, calm and collected. It wasn't much of a defence. . .in fact it was pretty pathetic. . .but she was determined not to give Matt the satisfaction of knowing that she was burning up with love and desire for him. She didn't have much left—but she did at least have her pride!

'Oh, my Gawd! What on earth is *that*?' Gloria exclaimed, as Francesca put a plate down in front of Ben.

'It's rum banana pancakes,' Ben told his wife firmly. 'And, before you start giving this sweet girl a hard time,' he added belligerently, before smiling up at Francesca, 'I may as well tell you that I particularly asked her to cook them for me this morning. OK?'

Francesca, who had briefly closed her eyes in anticipation of an hysterical outburst from Gloria, was amazed when the older woman merely murmured, 'Oh. . .well, in that case. . . I guess I may as well try some too.'

Although Ben looked easygoing, it was clear that Gloria wasn't prepared to push her husband around the way she did everyone else. Which must make Ben just about unique, Francesca told herself caustically.

'You can make some more for me as well,' Lois told her from the end of the table, where she was sitting next to Matt. And then, giving the English girl a simpering, malicious smile, she added, 'Matt and I had quite a lot of. . .um. . .*exercise* last night, didn't we, honey? So I guess that's why I've got such a *huge* appetite this morning!'

As Lois's throaty suggestive laugh rang around the room, Francesca threw a stricken glance down the table at the grim, taut lines of Matt's face. His hard, glittering emerald eyes met hers for a heart-stopping moment, before they both looked quickly away.

'I. . . I'll just go and—er. . .' Francesca mumbled, determined not to have to listen to whatever reply Matt had been going to make, as she hurried back into the galley.

She wasn't going to think about Matt and Lois's naked bodies lying together in the other girl's cabin last night—no, she *wasn't!* Francesca told herself fiercely. However, it took all the strength at her command to force herself to return to the saloon with a fresh batch of pancakes. Fortunately for her peace of mind, it seemed that the conversation had moved on from Matt and Lois's nocturnal sexual activities.

As she tried to concentrate on forcing some buttered toast and marmalade down her own throat, Francesca became aware that Lois had decided she'd had enough of Grenada.

'I don't see why we can't go somewhere else,' the other girl was saying in a petulant voice. 'I'm sure Dad would love to do some real sailing—wouldn't you?' She turned to smile winsomely at her father.

'Sure, anything you say, honey,' Ben agreed, before winking at Francesca as he poured some more rum sauce on his banana pancakes.

'Well—there you are, then.' Lois glanced triumphantly at Matt. 'How about Mustique? Gloria and I can't wait to go there. It sounds such an amazing place—a really fun island. In fact, I'm sure I remember reading somewhere that Mick Jagger *and* David Bowie have both built houses there too!'

'Hmm. . . I hear there are some divine parties—you'll be able to wear all those lovely clothes you bought,' Gloria chimed in enthusiastically. 'And don't forget that it's got sort of royal connections as well.' She turned to Francesca. 'Your Princess Margaret spends her holidays there, doesn't she?'

'I don't honestly know. . .'

Lois gave an incredulous, caustic laugh. 'What do you mean, you "don't know"? You *must* have read the gossip columns!'

'Why should I?' Francesca retorted icily. 'Frankly, I've got better things to do with my time,' she added, deciding that she was fed up to the back teeth with Matt's stupid girlfriend.

'Well—*really*!' Lois stiffened, tossing back her red hair with an angry gesture, her eyes flashing dangerously down the table at Francesca.

'I think we ought to wait a day or two,' Matt intervened smoothly. 'I'm not very happy about the weather, which looks just a little too overcast and windy. It can be a bit tricky sailing between here and the next island, Carriacou—and even then it's another thirty or so miles to Mustique.'

'Is that all?' Gloria exclaimed. 'It sounds like a nice day's sail to me.'

Matt gave her a sardonic smile. 'Not when the sea is as rough as I suspect it may well be!'

'Rough seas. . .?' Oh, well—maybe it's *not* such a good idea, after all,' Gloria murmured, clearly beginning to have second thoughts about the project.

'Oh, please, *do* say we can go, Matt,' Lois cried, ignoring her stepmother's sudden qualms. 'I thought this cruise was going to be fun. But we haven't gone anywhere—or done anything. I mean. . .it's all so *boring*!' she moaned, fluttering her long dark eyelashes up at Matt as she placed a hand pleadingly on his arm.

He gazed down at her for a moment with an inscrutable expression on his face, and then shrugged his broad shoulders. 'Well, OK—but don't say I didn't warn you that it may be a rough ride,' he drawled as he rose to his feet. 'I think I'd better get Calvin to run a check on the engine, just in case it's needed,' he added, before leaving the saloon.

'Hey—how about a cuppa coffee?' Calvin asked, putting his head around the door of the galley some two hours later. 'The boss ain't happy with the starter motor, and working on that engine sure is thirsty work!'

'Yes, of course,' Francesca said quickly, turning to grin at the man, whose face seemed to be covered with streaks of grease. 'Would you like something to eat? How about a cheese sandwich?' she added, concerned that he wasn't feeding himself properly.

Calvin, who always stayed on deck guarding the boat while Matt was below, took his meals in the galley. 'No problem!' he'd told Francesca when she'd questioned the arrangement. 'I reckon you meets a better class of

person in dis kitchen, anyway!' A remark which had
reduced them both to fits of laughter.

'Yeah, I reckon I could murder a cheese sandwich,'
he told her now. 'And I wouldn't mind one of those
small pizzas you made the other day if there's any left
in the freezer.'

'No problem!' she told him with a grin, suddenly
realising that, with Calvin on board, maybe the rest of
the cruise wouldn't be *all* doom and gloom.

Having made the basic preparations for lunch,
Francesca remembered that she hadn't yet changed the
linen in the guest rooms. In this sort of hot climate,
fresh sheets and towels every day were a must.
Although how she would have coped without the small
washing-machine and tumble-drier she had no idea.

Carrying a pile of linen through the saloon, towards
Ben and Gloria's large cabin at the front of the yacht,
she was halted in her tracks by the sound of Matt's
voice.

'Just a minute, Francesca,' he called out from where
he sat in front of the chart table, set in an alcove of the
large room.

Clutching the sheets and towels closely to her chest—
as if to ward off the evil eye—she walked reluctantly
and slowly towards him. The table was covered with
navigation charts, some rolled up while others lay flat
on the desk. As well as the normal VHF radio, with
which Matt kept in touch with his larger yacht *Wall
Street II* and their various ports of call around the
island, there was also a bewildering array of video
screens. Matt certainly believed in the application of
high tech on his yacht, she thought, looking bemusedly

at a coloured screen, which seemed to be showing some sort of radar plotting system.

Matt spun around on his swivel chair, staring for some moments at the girl standing nervously before him. 'Did you eat any breakfast?' he asked abruptly.

'No. . .no, I didn't,' she muttered, frowning slightly at him in puzzlement. Whatever she'd thought he might be going to say, it certainly hadn't been about her appetite! 'Well. . .only a slice of toast. Why?'

'I wasn't joking about the first part of the voyage being a bit rough,' he explained. 'I've just heard a weather report on the radio, and they've announced that there's a tropical depression with sustained winds of up to thirty-five knots and a rainstorm coming our way.' He shrugged. 'It's certainly not dangerous—although Kick 'em Jenny can produce a nasty sea, particularly if the tide is running east—which it is.'

'Kick 'em Jenny. . .?'

He turned bck towards an open chart lying on the table. Pointing a brown finger at a small collection of islands off the north coast of Grenada, he said, 'Strong currents, eddies and rip-tides swirl around and between these islands. Kick 'em Jenny is the most northerly one, and, though small, it can kick up a nasty sea. Hence the name!' he added with a grin.

Interested despite herself, Francesca leaned forward to gaze down at the navigation chart, which she found bewilderingly covered in a mass of lines and circles. 'Why do you get swirling currents there?' she asked.

He shrugged his shoulders. 'There are the normal sea currents, of course, but what gives this area a particular interest is that there's an underwater volcano here, off the Sisters.' Once again he pointed at the map, indicating three small dots to the left of the clutch of islands.

'Is it dangerous?'

'No, not really. But, as I said, it is likely to be rough sailing for a while. Especially with this depression on its way. So I thought I'd better warn you that, since you aren't used to boats and sailing, there is a chance of your being seasick. Although not having eaten too much at breakfast should stand you in good stead.'

'Well—er—thank you for warning me,' she muttered, surprised by his unexpected kindness and concern.

Realising that she must get on with her work, she turned away, only to be stopped as he reached up and caught hold of her elbow.

'Just a minute,' he said. 'We've still got a lot of things to thrash out between us.'

'I. . . I'm far too busy,' she muttered, trying to tug herself away from his firm grasp. 'Please, Matt—let me go,' she pleaded as he stood up, still maintaining his grip on her arm.

'There have obviously been far too many misunderstandings between us. So, when we get to Mustique, I intend to have a long serious talk to you,' he said firmly.

'Oh, yes?' Her soft lips tightened. 'As far as I'm concerned, you've already said—and done—quite enough! Why don't you just concentrate on dear Lois?' she added waspishly. 'From what she said at breakfast, you both seemed to have had a great "conversation" late last night!'

He gave her a mocking grin. 'I can assure you that, despite what Lois might say, we merely had a cool dip in the sea before retiring to our—er—separate cabins.'

'What you did or didn't do is a matter of supreme indifference to me,' she said woodenly, trying to ignore the tall figure looming over her.

'Really?' A small amused smile played about his lips as he gazed down at her flushed cheeks and trembling figure. 'However, I meant what I said just now. It's important that you and I spend some time together.'

'In your bed, I suppose?' she rasped angrily.

'I certainly hope so!' He gave a low rumble of sardonic laughter as he pulled her closer to his tall figure. 'Maybe not *all* the time, but——'

'No way!' she gasped, struggling to free herself. She could feel her bones melting at his close proximity, the touch of his cool fingers as he put his hand beneath her chin, tilting her head up towards him.

His glittering emerald eyes bored down into hers, and she felt as though her brain were being probed by a sharp, icy-cold scalpel. She was suddenly and startlingly aware of the faint flush beneath his tanned skin, stretched tightly over his high cheekbones and formidable jaw, the cruel sensuality of his lips.

'Don't try and fool me—or yourself,' he told her softly, although it was impossible for her to miss the underlying threat and menace in his quite voice. 'This is neither the right time, nor the right place. But it doesn't alter the fact that *you* want me—and *I* fully intend to have you!'

'You. . .you arrogant swine!' she cried, before hearing the sound of footsteps beginning to descend the companion-way which led down into the saloon. Furiously tearing her arm away from his slackening grip, she bolted towards Gloria's cabin. 'I'll see you in hell first!' she hissed through clenched teeth, before quickly slamming the door behind her.

Unfortunately, her Parthian shot did not achieve its aim. Her ears seemed to be filled with the rumble of his sardonic laughter, clearly audible through the closed door. As her trembling legs gave way beneath her, she sank down on to the bed, the frantic hammering of her heart beating a loud tattoo throughout her quivering body.

'Cast off for'ard! Raise the mainsail!'

Francesca climbed up into the main cockpit at the rear of the yacht, carrying some cans of beer and a large plate of sandwiches. Placing them carefully down on the top of a locker, she leaned against the side of the hull, gazing over at Matt's tall figure.

Staring at the long brown legs and bronze chest of the man who was wearing only a pair of brief white shorts, she could feel her heart give a sudden sickening lurch. He looks. . .he looks magnificent! she acknowledged reluctantly to herself, watching silently as he stood easily balanced on the rear deck, calling out his commands in a loud, staccato voice that demanded immediate obedience.

After giving herself a strong talking to, Francesca had convinced herself that if she didn't keep over-reacting to Matt he might well stop trying to wind her up. And, with a possibly dangerous storm ahead of them, she was just going to have to put her private feelings on the back burner for the time being.

Although their departure had been originally timed for mid-morning, there had been a long delay because of problems with the engine. 'We may need it—if only to get us out of trouble,' Matt had announced, firmly refusing to abandon his careful preparations, despite the continual pressure from Lois to do so.

Unlike her stepdaughter, Gloria had become increasingly nervous throughout the morning. Both she and Francesca had taken heed of Matt's dire warnings about the weather and, like Francesca, Gloria clearly wasn't looking forward to the voyage. It was only the thought of arriving at the up-market island of Mustique—and being able to rub shoulders with some of its jet-set inhabitants—that was keeping her going, she'd confided.

'And no lunch for me,' Gloria had added firmly. 'Just thinking about a rough sea is enough to make me feel queasy.'

Believe me—you're not the only one! Francesca had been thinking, when she'd been startled by a shout from up on deck.

'*Raise the anchor!*'

Gloria's cheeks had paled as she'd heard Matt's loud disembodied voice calling out instructions on the upper deck and the indistinct replies from Ben and Calvin, accompanied by the sound of the heavy anchor-chain being wound up into its locker.

'I never wanted to come on this damn cruise—and I'd give *anything* to be back on dry land!' the older woman had moaned, looking up as Calvin had put his head through one of the hatches above their heads.

'The boss says he wants a whole lot of BLTs and some beer,' he'd announced, before quickly disappearing from sight.

'What on earth's a BLT?' Francesca frowned.

'A bacon, lettuce and tomato sandwich,' Gloria had told her, before groaning aloud at the thought of food and disappearing into her cabin.

Standing up on deck now, Francesca was surprised to find herself feeling sorry for the older woman. Despite the past few days, during which Gloria had made her life a total misery, it was obvious that Ben's wife really was dead scared of sailing on the open sea. And I'm not too mad on it myself, she thought as she watched the final preparations for departure.

To her inexperienced eyes, their exit from the bay seemed chaotic and confused, but she had no doubt that Matt knew exactly what he was doing. It soon became equally clear that he was very much the captain of the boat—and not prepared to brook any interference whatsoever. He certainly had Ben's and Calvin's full attention. The two men were obviously working flat out, as they quickly jumped to attention and instantly complied with his orders.

'Ease the sheet! *Ease the sheet!*' Matt bellowed repeatedly as Calvin struggled to free part of the sail, which had got caught up in the rigging.

'Watch the dinghy!' he shouted to Francesca as he started the engine. And when she stared at him, nonplussed, she found herself thrust roughly aside. A second later he was adjusting the long thick nylon rope which lay in the water between *Silver Lady* and the small boat floating some yards away.

'For goodness' sake, sit down!' he snapped at her, before leaping to take hold of the wheel.

'I'm willing to help if I can——'

'Sit down—and shut up!' he barked, quickly turning the yacht into the wind before calling out to Calvin, 'That's enough sheet!'

'You're just a. . .a damn Captain Ahab,' she grumbled, sinking down on to a small built-in bench-seat as she recalled Herman Melville's book *Moby-Dick*, the story of a tragic voyage under the mad, obsessive Captain Ahab in pursuit of a whale. But Matt merely laughed and shouted at Ben to keep a watch on the dangerous reef off their port bow.

Leaning back and watching the hectic activity as the elegant schooner began moving through the water, Francesca began to appreciate some people's mania for boats and the sea. The early clouds had now disappeared, and it was a wonderfully hot, clear day. As the yacht gathered speed, lightly skimming over the sparkling blue water, she could understand how sailing might well become an addiction.

'Right—things seem to have calmed down a bit,' Matt said, keeping a hand on the wheel as he reached down to help himself to a sandwich. 'How is everyone down below?'

'I haven't seen Lois for a while, and Gloria has retired to her cabin,' she told him.

'The best place for her!' he grinned. 'How are you feeling?'

'Well. . .surprisingly enough, I'm feeling quite OK.'

She looked around at the peaceful scene. 'Are you *sure* that there's going to be a storm? It seems almost impossible—especially as there isn't a cloud in the sky.'

He shrugged. 'You can never be certain of anything, in these waters. But if Radio Antilles is forecasting a tropical depression in zone three—that's the Windward Islands—it's as well to be prepared. However, I can practically guarantee a rough sea around Kick 'em Jenny. So you've got about an hour to serve lunch to the others before taking to your bed like Gloria!' he added, quickly spinning the wheel as Calvin called out, warning about a coral reef ahead.

'Well. . . I suppose I'd better get on with the cooking,' she sighed.

Even though it was a bit scary up here on deck—especially the way the yacht seemed to be tilting dangerously over as it skimmed across the waves—she was strangely reluctant to go down below. On the other hand, she couldn't think of a good reason to stay up here any longer. And she *definitely* didn't want Matt to think that she was interested in his company.

'Just make sure you keep me supplied with plenty of coffee and sandwiches,' he called out as she began making her way down into the saloon.

'A woman's work is never done—not when there's a male chauvinist pig like you around!' she muttered.

He laughed. 'Ah. . .but you know that you love me really!'

'*No*! I certainly do *not*!' she snapped, swearing violently under her breath as she stumped into the galley, slamming the louvred door violently behind her.

Kick 'em Jenny more than lived up to its reputation. Francesca had just finished serving lunch to Ben, Calvin and Lois—Gloria, very sensibly, having decided to forgo the meal—when the yacht began to rise and fall in a thoroughly alarming manner. However, when she took Matt up a mug of coffee—losing half of the liquid before even handing it to him, thanks to the boat's turbulent motion—she almost wished she hadn't. Huge waves were breaking over the schooner, and she noticed a large dark cloud on the horizon.

'Yes, I'm afraid we're out of luck,' Matt said and confirmed her worst fears, which were magnified as she watched him attach a safety-line to a belt around his waist, clipping the other end to the guard rail.

'It's only a sensible precaution,' he told her soothingly. 'It wouldn't do for the skipper to be swept overboard—would it?' he added with a short bark of laughter.

Francesca, for her part, could see no humour in the situation. 'For goodness' sake—do be careful, Matt,' she begged anxiously, clinging tightly to a rail as a large wave washed over the hull.

'Of course I will,' he assured her, seemingly ignoring the cold spray which had drenched his tall figure. 'I have *no* intention of going to Kingdom Come just yet anyway—and certainly not before I've made love to you!' he added with a wolfish grin.

'You'll be lucky!' she ground out, before flinching nervously as another wave smashed into the cockpit, leaving her almost as wet as he was.

'Luck has nothing to do with it! However, I think we'd better concentrate on the here and now for the time being.' He gave her a sardonic smile. 'I reckon the storm will hit us in about half an hour—maybe less. So check with Calvin that all the hatches are well battened down, and then tell him that I want Ben to take the wheel while he gives me a hand with reefing in the sails. Got that?'

'Aye, aye, *Captain*!' she muttered through chattering teeth, her body shivering with the cold—and with fear. 'We. . .we are going to be all right, aren't we?'

'No problem—as Calvin would say!' he grinned. 'Compared to the Atlantic, this is a piece of cake.'

It may have been a piece of cake for Matt—but, as far as Francesca was concerned, the next few hours were sheer, unadulterated hell.

Even with the hatches firmly closed against the storm outside, every time a wave broke over the bow of the yacht the sound was magnified so that it sounded like a heavy sledge-hammer beating against the hull. Francesca was frightened almost out of her wits, but she had little or no time to dwell on her fears. The demands of everyone else on board soon saw to that!

Ben, who'd been sent below by Matt, primarily to have a brief rest—in case the storm lasted a long time and he had to take the wheel from Matt—demanded a hot cup of soup before going to lie down in the spare cabin, opposite that occupied by Lois. And no sooner had she forced herself to heat up a can of tomato soup—an extremely difficult manoeuvre since the yacht seemed to be going up and down like a lift—when her attention was claimed by his wife and daughter.

Gloria, who had already taken to her bed, quickly gave up the ghost, crying and screaming with hysterics until she began to be violently sick. Lois had also disappeared into her cabin. Swiftly succumbing to the boat's turbulent motion, she clung tightly to her bunk, issuing loud moans and groans until she became as ill as her stepmother. As the rough plunging motion of the yacht increased, Calvin helped Francesca to tie restraining lengths of wide tape around the two women's comatose figures.

'That'll stop 'em rolling off the bunks,' Calvin said as he followed her into the galley, where she began filling a bucket with water to clear up the mess in the cabins.

'I think they're over the worst,' Francesca said, wearily brushing the damp hair from her brow. 'I wish it weren't so hot and stifling down here with all the hatches closed. How long do you think it will be before we're through the storm?'

Calvin shrugged his shoulders. 'I ain't sure. But we is quite safe with the boss at the helm.'

'I hope so,' she muttered fervently, bracing herself against the sink as the yacht seemed to rise and then plunge deeply into the sea. 'How—er——' she gulped nervously as the boat regained an even keel '—how is Matt? Is he going to be all right?' She cast a frightened glance up at the deck above their heads.

'No problem!' Calvin told her reassuringly. 'You don't look too bad, either,' he added, eyeing the girl who, despite her wan face, was surprisingly still on her feet.

'Don't be fooled—I feel *ghastly*!' Francesca told him with a grim smile, emptying a large amount of disinfectant into the bucket. 'Fortunately—or unfortunately, depending on how you look at it—I don't seem to have had any time to be ill. If it's not Gloria screaming blue murder, it's Lois who's convinced she's at death's door,' she said with a sigh, lifting the bucket out of the small sink and making her way back to clean up the cabins.

It wasn't until she had done all she could for the other two women that Francesca felt she could seek the refuge of her own cabin. Goodness knows why she hadn't been seasick, she thought, falling exhausted on to her bed. Maybe she had been right when she'd told Calvin that she'd just been too darn busy to be ill. . .

When she eventually surfaced some hours later it was to find the boat lying calm and still in the water. Expecting to be feeling really dreadful, she was amazed to find that she didn't. In fact, other than wishing she could let some fresh air into the hot, stuffy cabin, she felt remarkably well. However, as she obviously hadn't descended to a watery grave, maybe she ought to get up and see if she could help the others?

Miraculously, it seemed possible to have a shower. 'Bad luck, Lois—it's *my* turn!' she muttered as she shampooed her hair, before groaning with pleasure beneath the fine needle-spray of cold water. After changing into a cool aquamarine version of the shorts, with their matching T-shirt, that she'd put on that morning, and thoroughly brushing her long wet hair, Francesca decided that she definitely felt a new woman.

The yacht seemed deserted as she made her way through the saloon and up on to the deck. But, as she stood blinking in the strong late-afternoon sunlight, she was startled to hear a voice behind her.

'Well, well. . .*well*! Good old Matt—I ought to have known that he'd have a gorgeous girl on board!'

Spinning around, she saw Matt leaning casually against the rail of the yacht, and, standing beside him, a remarkably handsome fair-haired man.

'Behave yourself—this is my stepsister,' Matt told him sternly. 'Francesca, I'd like you to meet James Fielding, who is a thoroughly disreputable old schoolfriend of mine. If you've got any sense you won't trust him an inch!'

The man laughed as he walked across the deck. 'Pure slander!' he drawled, his startling blue eyes glinting with amusement. 'Unfortunately, Matt's never forgiven me for stealing his first girlfriend from him when we were at Eton.'

'Hello, James. . .' she murmured, feeling slightly dazed as he took her hand, raising it gallantly to his lips.

'And hello to *you*, Francesca!' he murmured back, his frank appreciation bringing a flush to her cheeks. 'How come I've never met this simply *wonderful* girl before now?' James demanded, keeping hold of her hand as he turned towards Matt. 'I think I'm in love!'

'I warned you!' Matt told her with a grim smile.

'Er—where exactly are we? And where are Calvin and the Wagners?' she murmured, gazing around at the other boats, anchored alongside them in a wide curving bay.

'Calvin's gone ashore for provisions, and all the Wagners are down below, dead to the world,' Matt explained. 'This is Tyrrel Bay, on the island of Carriacou. I ran in here for shelter during the storm.'

'I couldn't believe my luck when I saw *Silver Lady*,' James said, still keeping a firm grip on her hand. 'I was island-hopping up to Mustique when they closed the small airport here. And then, just as I was drowning my sorrows in that bar over there. . .' he gestured towards a small row of shops and cafés beside the road edging the sandy bay '. . .dear old Matt sailed into town!'

'Hmm. . ."dear old Matt" now thinks he might have made a bad mistake,' his old school-friend told him, casting a far from friendly glance at James's hand, still firmly clasping that of Francesca.

James grinned. 'Nonsense! And, since I've fallen hook, line and sinker for your beautiful stepsister, I'm delighted to be able to cadge a lift with you to Mustique. Frankly, Matt, I don't just think I'm in love—I *know* that I am!' he laughed.

'Oh, *really*?'

Francesca's cheeks flushed as she caught both the deep, underlying tension in Matt's lazy drawl and the ice-cold glint in his green eyes. It was clear to her, if not to James, that Matthew Sinclair appeared to have suddenly lost his sense of humour.

CHAPTER EIGHT

BOISTEROUS shrieks of laughter and the high-pitched, noisy babble of conversation filled the hot, humid evening air.

Trying to compete against the loud exuberant music of the band, playing out on the small dance-floor under the stars, made it almost impossible to hold a conversation, Francesca thought as James led her into the relative calm of the bar. Built out on stilts over the waters of Britannia Bay, Basils Bar and Restaurant certainly seemed to be the 'in' place on Mustique.

'This is a typical Wednesday night "jump-up",' James told her, still having to raise his voice against the deafening sound of so many people crowded into a small area.

'Does everyone come here?' she asked, casting a nervous look around the bar. 'I mean, I don't want to bump into Matt, and. . .'

'Relax!' James grinned. 'Matt's supposed to be having dinner with the Wagners, isn't he? And I know that he's also busy arranging for Calvin to get home.'

'Calvin? Where does he live?'

James shrugged. 'Calvin comes from Bequia—an island not very far away from here. I'm not sure how he and Matt originally got together. But, as you know, Matt owns a house somewhere on one of these small islands, and so. . .'

'No, I didn't know that,' she told him with a puzzled frown.

'Didn't you? James's eyebrows rose in surprise. 'I know he keeps its location pretty dark—even I haven't a clue where it is. Apparently, he calls it his secret hideaway, and I don't know any of his friends who've been invited there. But I was sure *you'd* know about it, especially as you're his—er—his stepsister,' he added lamely.

She shook her head. 'No. We've never had that sort of close relationship,' she told him wryly, before quickly deciding to say no more on the subject.

James was obviously keen to know the whereabouts of the house, and clearly Matt didn't trust his old school-friend—any more than he trusted her. So what's new? Francesca asked herself glumly. Matt never *had* trusted her, so he was hardly likely to start doing so now, was he?

'Anyway, who wants to talk about Matt all night?' James was saying. 'How about some of Basil's special rum punch?'

'Yes. . .that sounds like a good idea,' Francesca told him, trying to sound a good deal more enthusiastic than she felt.

As she watched James making his way towards the bar, she felt guilty at not being able to be a more sparkling companion. Although Matt's friend was extraordinarily good-looking and great company, the past two days had been so traumatic that she seemed to be in a constant state of nervous tension.

For once it *wasn't* the Wagners' fault. Both Lois and Gloria, when they had eventually recovered from their serious bout of seasickness, had flatly refused to stay one more night on Matt's yacht.

'You can do what you like, honey,' Gloria had told her husband, 'but Lois and I have *had it*!' Insisting that Ben immediately take her and her stepdaughter to the small airport on Carriacou so that they could fly direct to Mustique, Gloria had also commanded her husband to get them rooms in the Cotton House, the only hotel on that island.

'I don't know how I'm going to be able to do that,' Ben had confided to Francesca, having made it clear that he himself had every intention of staying on board. 'Matt was dead certain that the place is likely to be completely full at this time of year. He says it's a waste of time even trying to raise the hotel on the VHF.'

However, although Matt had pointed out to Gloria and Lois that there were far more hotels and many more things to do on the adjacent island of Bequia, the American women had made their minds up: it was either Mustique or they were going straight back to New York!

Francesca had been surprised that Lois, once she'd recovered from her bout of seasickness, had decided to leave *Silver Lady*. The other girl had clearly fancied being Mrs Matthew Sinclair—so why wasn't she staying on board, where she could be in close contact with Matt? Although maybe it was her determination to join Gloria on Mustique which was the reason why Matt was clearly so against the idea of their staying on the island.

However, and despite Matt's strong opposition, it appeared that James had some influential friends on

Mustique. Contacting them via the VHF radio—when Matt had been ashore, dealing with the customs authorities in Carriacou—he had arranged for the Wagners to rent a private house, complete with swimming-pool, tennis court, a bevy of servants and two cars.

'That's more like it!' Gloria had announced with satisfaction, even going so far—now that she was leaving the yacht—to thank Francesca for looking after her when she'd been so ill.

'Why don't you come with us?' Lois had asked James, giving the handsome man one of her brilliant megawatt smiles as she and Gloria had prepared to leave for the airport.

'Yes, why *don't* you?' Matt had drawled smoothly, the bland expression on his face tightening as James had merely laughed, before settling himself more comfortably on a couch in the saloon.

'No, thanks. I'm quite comfortable where I am.' James grinned up at his old school-friend. 'Besides, I have no intention of leaving your lovely cook to languish alone on this boat, and——'

'I'm fine, really,' Francesca quickly intervened, disturbed by the strong undercurrent of animosity between the two men.

'Sure she is,' Lois agreed, tossing her long red hair back from her lovely face. 'Come on, James. We could have a lot of fun!'

'And, since Ben and I are remaining on board, Francesca will hardly be alone,' Matt pointed out tersely.

James shook his head, clearly refusing to bow down to their combined pressure. 'All of you should be ashamed of yourselves,' he said sternly. 'As far as I can see, this gorgeous girl has been used as nothing more or less than a drudge. I've decided to do what I can to brighten up her life,' he added, blithely ignoring the increasingly tight-lipped, angry expression on Matt's face.

Francesca's heart sank as Lois glared angrily at her before stalking furiously out of the saloon. Matt was already in an inexplicably foul mood, and she *really* didn't need his friend making matters far worse.

'In fact, I mean to start right away,' James continued, jumping up and quickly taking hold of Francesca's hand. 'Come on, lovely. Let's leave these boring people and go and explore down-town Hillsborough!'

Caught totally by surprise at his action, Francesca found herself being rapidly propelled up the companion-way before she had a chance to protest at James's action. And after he had bundled her into the speedboat, which he'd hired to bring him out to *Silver Lady*, she'd hardly been able to catch her breath before she found herself standing on the jetty.

'Matt's going to be *furious!*' she told James as he hailed a passing taxi.

'Yes, I rather think he is!' James agreed with a mischievous grin, resolutely refusing to discuss the matter any further until they had toured the small town, and were having a cool drink on the terrace of the Casada Bay Hotel.

'It's lovely here,' Francesca sighed, gazing out over the shimmering blue water towards some small deserted islands off shore. 'I just wish. . .' She paused, and gave another heavy sigh.

'Look here. . .' James gave her a warm smile. 'I don't know what game Matt thinks he's playing, but I can't help feeling you're an idiot to put up with any of his nonsense. Why you should be scrubbing the decks and cooking nineteen to the dozen, when he can well afford a whole battery of French chefs, completely beats me!'

'Well. . .' Francesca hesitated before beginning to tell him all about her agreement with Matt.

James raised a sceptical eyebrow. 'Oh—come on! Are you seriously trying to tell me that he wouldn't help you to get hold of your own money? Not unless you agreed to cook and act as stewardess on that yacht of his. . .?' And when she nodded dumbly he shook his head in disbelief. 'The whole affair sounds very odd to me. Although I'll tell you one thing: ever since I came aboard the yacht he's been acting towards me like some jealous husbands of my acquaintance! My guess is that he fancies you rotten!'

Francesca shrugged, her cheeks flushing as she told him, 'He's intending to marry Lois.'

'Do me a favour!' James roared with laughter. 'I've only just met the girl, but even *I* know a spoilt brat when I see one! Besides, Matt was obviously deeply relieved to get her—and that awful stepmother of hers—off the boat.

'No,' he continued, after giving the matter some thought, 'no, I reckon that, even if he isn't aware of the fact, Matt is crazy about you. And, since you're obviously equally crazy about him—I shall have to see whether I can help matters along!'

'Oh, for goodness' sake—*please* don't get involved,'

she begged urgently. 'It's. . .it's all a bit complicated. . .but the fact is, Matt doesn't really give tuppence about me—not *me* as a person. And half the time I'm not sure that I don't hate the horrid man! I've only got to stagger through a few more days, and then I can go back to London. Quite honestly,' she added wearily, 'I've got past the point of caring whether I get hold of the art gallery or not. I just want to grab hold of my passport. . .and go home!'

But, of course, James *had* got involved, Francesca thought gloomily. Sitting here now in Basil's Bar, watching James as he continued to keep trying to catch the bartender's attention, she shuddered as she recalled the overwhelming stress and strains of their voyage from Carriacou to Mustique. The hostile, tense atmosphere, which had increasingly pervaded the yacht over the past two days, had become almost unbearable.

How or why James had imagined that blatantly flirting with her would somehow help matters she had no idea. Ben had more or less managed to keep the two old school-friends from coming to blows, but it had been touch and go for much of the time.

As for Matt. . .there was only one word to describe his behaviour—hellish! Aggressive, belligerent and truculent by turn, he seemed to snap and shout at everyone—everyone, that was, except Francesca. For her he reserved an icy silence that was far more unnerving than anything he could have said or done.

If it hadn't been for Ben Wagner, she was convinced that she'd have gone clear out of her mind. He'd been incredibly kind and supportive, pathetically grateful for all the help and assistance she'd given to Gloria and

Lois when they'd been so seasick, and genuinely interested in her plans for the art gallery.

'It has to be a good buy,' he'd told her. 'As you know, I was in the real-estate business for some years, and I guess those sort of buildings in Bond Street don't come on to the market very often. So, even if it costs you an arm and a leg, you've got to go for it—right? All the same,' he'd added, 'I reckon you'd better get back and seal the deal real quick. I can think of several companies who'd give their eye-teeth for a property like that.'

Francesca had realised that Ben was absolutely right—she ought to sign a contract with Oscar Thornton as soon as possible. However, when she'd tried to talk to her stepbrother to find out whether the fax he'd sent for her could be regarded as a firm offer for the property, Matt wouldn't even discuss the subject. Just as he had tried to prevent her from taking a break tonight from all her duties on board the yacht.

Although she ought to have known better, she hadn't been able to believe he really meant it. 'You can't be serious,' she'd laughed nervously. 'All I want is just *one* evening away from the galley, for heaven's sake! Surely that's not too much to ask?'

But it seemed that it was.

'Your place is here, on board this boat,' he'd told her sternly.

'Look, I've cooked and cleaned. . .and done all that you've asked me to,' she'd said in as reasonable a tone as she could manage. 'You and Ben are joining Lois and Gloria for a meal ashore. So, with no one to cook for, there's no earthly reason why I can't join James for a drink, is there?'

'I'm not prepared to discuss the matter any further,' Matt had retorted in a cold, hard voice. 'You will stay here, on *Silver Lady*—and that's my last word on the subject!'

Well, it might have been *his* last word, but it certainly wasn't *hers*! she'd thought mutinously. Determined to disregard the awful man's quite unreasonable demand—why should she have to stay alone on the yacht while everyone else was away enjoying themselves?—Francesca had told James that she would meet him at Basils Bar later that evening. And then, with the help and connivance of Calvin, who'd laughingly agreed to pick her up in the dinghy once Matt had gone safely ashore, she'd stormed down into her cabin.

Maybe it hadn't been a terribly good idea to put on this crazy dress, Francesca thought now, glancing down at the glittering silver and gold sequins covering the *very* tight-fitting, almost indecently short, sexy garment. Even if it was a couture model by a very famous designer—she'd practically had hysterics on reading the label after sobering up from her mad shopping spree in St George's—it still wasn't her sort of dress. And, even if Matt was as rich as Croesus, he was bound to be *very* angry when he discovered just how much it was going to cost him!

However, if she'd wanted to attract attention she'd certainly succeeded! James had given her one amazed, stunned glance before clearing his throat and giving vent to a loud wolf-whistle. 'You're going to be driving the men up the wall tonight,' he'd told her, adding with a rueful laugh, 'and I'm not sure that I'm going to be able to keep my hands off you, either!'

Since she wasn't romantically interested in James— and he knew it—she'd merely laughed at his reaction. However, she was now beginning to think that she had been a bit of an idiot. James had been right—she *had* created a minor sensation! Under normal circumstances, she might have enjoyed being the subject of some considerable attention. But that hadn't been the object of the exercise, had it? If she was to be honest, the only point in wearing this awful dress had been to annoy Matt. . .the very *last* person she wanted to see tonight. So why on earth had she dressed in something that made her stand out like a sore thumb?

Quickly deciding not to delve any further into the murky depths of the confusing, complicated motivation behind her defiant gesture, Francesca was startled to hear Gloria's familiar strident voice hailing her from across the room.

'Well—if it isn't little Fran-*ches*-ca!' she shrieked above the din, rushing over to sink gratefully down into James's vacant chair. 'Thank Gawd! I've been dying to put my feet up! It's murder trying to walk on the sand,' she moaned, slipping off a high-heeled sandal and rubbing her toes.

Where Gloria was, Matt and Lois couldn't be far behind, Francesca realised, her stomach clenching nervously as she looked quickly around the crowded bar. She couldn't see Matt anywhere, but she had a sinking feeling that her luck wasn't going to hold out much longer.

'We're all absolutely enchanted with this darling island!' Gloria was saying, as Francesca tried to pull herself together. 'I've seen *so* many famous people— although I'm not always quite sure of their names,' the older woman confided. 'And as for the boutiques here! Well, the clothes are simply *out* of this world—Lois and I must have spent a *fortune*!' she laughed happily. 'I tell you—it's really my sort of place!'

'Oh—er—good,' Francesca mumbled, not really listening to Gloria as her eyes continued to flick nervously about the room. 'Er—talking of Lois. . .is she here tonight?'

'Oh, sure. I expect she's on the dance-floor right now. Lois is having an *amazing* time—quite swept off her feet by all the attention she's been getting! And how are you, dear? Hey—that's some dress you're wearing, huh?' Gloria laughed.

Francesca blinked at the older woman's warm and friendly attitude towards her. It was probably unfair, but she couldn't help wondering why Gloria had suddenly decided to be so nice. She soon had the answer.

'I didn't realise. . . I never dreamed that Matt was your *stepbrother*!' the American woman continued, a slightly querulous note in her voice as she gave the younger girl a sickly smile. 'I can't think why he didn't tell us. It. . .well, it would have saved so many—er— misunderstandings, if you see what I mean?'

Francesca shrugged. What was there to say? She could hardly tell this woman that she'd been blackmailed into serving as chef on the yacht. And that she was as mystified as Gloria about the reason why Matt hadn't told everyone about their family connection. 'When did he tell you?' she asked.

'Well, he told Lois, actually. I think they were having a little disagreement at the time. You know how it is. . .' Gloria gave her another slightly guilty smile. 'I think dear Lois has been just a little bit jealous of you, and——'

'Jealous? Of *me*?' Francesca looked at her in amazement. 'Lois is—far and away—one of the most outstandingly beautiful girls I've ever seen!'

'Yes, she is beautiful, isn't she?' Gloria agreed with a fond smile. 'I must admit,' she lowered her voice, 'I was hoping that Matt and Lois. . .' She broke off, raising her head to give a beaming smile at someone behind Francesca. 'Ah. . .here is dear James with the drinks,' she murmured before raising her hand and waving across the room. 'That looks like dear Matt over there,' she added happily. 'How nice for us all to meet up like this!'

'Nice' is *not* the word I'd have chosen, Francesca thought grimly, closing her eyes for a moment and taking a deep breath as she prepared for the worst.

'A little drinkie for me, too? How sweet of you, James,' Gloria cooed as he placed a tray on the table. 'I was just saying what fun it is for us all to be together again.'

'Yes, isn't it?' James agreed blandly, turning his head to wink at Francesca. 'I hope the house you've taken is proving to be comfortable?'

'Oh, it's just *perfect*! You must come over and spend some time with us. We'd love to see Matt too, of course. In fact, we'd been hoping he was going to have dinner with us tonight. But he couldn't make it for some reason. Lois was *very* disappointed. However, we're all having such fun, and the servants have been so helpful. . .'

'Gloria's just said that she's seen Matt *here*!' Francesca hissed at James out of the corner of her mouth as the older woman continued to enthuse loudly about the many advantages of renting a house, as opposed to staying in a hotel. 'He's bound to be absolutely *furious* when he sees me. What on earth am I going to do?' Francesca added in an urgent whisper.

'Don't panic!' James murmured before cutting ruthlessly into Gloria's non-stop chatter. 'I do hope you'll excuse us. . .' he gave the older woman a charming smile as he stood up '. . .but I've promised to have a dance with Francesca.'

'Oh, sure—have fun, kids,' Gloria told them. 'I'll just sit here and see how many celebrities I can spot!' she added with a happy laugh.

'Well done, James!' Francesca breathed with relief as he led her on to the crowded dance-floor, set out on the beach under the stars. 'I've had as much confrontation as I can take over these last few days!'

'Hmm. . . Matt hasn't been in the best of moods, has he?' James grinned as he took her loosely into his arms.

'No—he certainly hasn't! And it's been mostly your fault,' she told him accusingly.

James laughed. 'All's fair in love and war!'

'But you don't love me,' she muttered with exasperation. 'And neither does Matt. . .she added miserably to herself.

'Don't kid yourself,' James said roughly. 'Matt may be a fool—but I'm not! If you gave me half a chance I could fall for you like a ton of bricks. As it is. . .' He gave a heavy sigh, pulling her closer to him.

James was a really nice man, she thought unhappily as they continued to dance silently together. It seemed grotesque somehow to be out here, beneath the soft moonlight, in the arms of a man for whom she felt absolutely nothing. This was surely a night made for lovers. . .

Her confused thoughts were sharply interrupted as a hand was suddenly placed firmly on James's shoulder.

'Excuse me,' Matt drawled, 'but I think it's now *my* turn to dance with this indecently dressed girl!'

'Hey—just a minute!' James protested as Matt swiftly grasped her wrist, spinning her around into his arms. 'Francesca's here with me.'

'Really?' Matt murmured coolly. 'Well, I'm sure that dear Gloria will be happy to entertain you until we've finished our dance,' he added smoothly. Giving his friend a bland, ruthless smile, he quickly pulled Francesca away into the crowd.

'What do you think you're doing?' she demanded angrily. 'I'm here with James, and——'

'Why don't you just shut up and dance?' he said grimly, leading her to the far side of the floor, beside the waves lapping against the shore of the bay.

'I don't want to dance with you,' she retorted. 'Anyway, I thought you were with Lois, and——' Her angry words were swiftly cut off as Matt's mouth descended on her open lips in a firm, determined kiss.

'I don't want any more nonsense,' he threatened

harshly, staring down into her dazed eyes. 'So why don't you keep quiet and let's dance, hmm?'

'I really hate you!' she spat, unwilling to cause a scene—a fact of which he was well aware, she thought furiously.

'Hate? Oh, no—I don't think so!' he murmured softly, smiling cynically down into her angry blue eyes. Putting his arms about her, he slowly drew her closer and closer.

Trying hard to keep herself stiff and unyielding, Francesca was unable to prevent her treacherous body from slowly responding to the sensual mood of the music, and to the firm figure pressed so closely to her own. Shivers of excitement began to run down her spine, and she trembled as Matt placed his cheek to hers, softly pressing his warm lips to her brow.

As they continued to sway to the music, he lowered his head, his mouth brushing hers with a gentle, sensually erotic touch that sent the blood pulsing rapidly through her veins. His mouth teased and tantalised her lips until she was breathless, her heart thudding in her breast as she quivered helplessly in his arms.

I've got to get out of here! she told herself, desperately trying to cling on to some sort of sanity. But, even as she framed the thought, Matt's lips abruptly left hers.

'Come on,' he growled, clasping hold of her wrist in a grip of steel as he swiftly towed her off the dance-floor towards the car park at the rear of the property.

'Where are we going?' she cried, still feeling completely dazed by their intimate embrace. He didn't reply until a few moments later, when they came to a halt beside a low open sports car.

'In you get,' he commanded, opening the passenger door.

'Where. . .where are you taking me?' she asked nervously, desperately wishing—when it was clearly far too late—that she'd obeyed his orders and remained on board *Silver Lady*.

'We're going to my house, of course,' he said impatiently. 'Where else?'

'How would I know?' she snapped nervously. 'I don't want to go *anywhere*—and especially not with you!' she added mutinously as he continued to hold the door open.

Matt's lips tightened. Without any warning he swept her up in his arms and roughly dumped her down on the seat in one fluid movement before slamming the door shut and going around to the other side of the vehicle.

Francesca sat where he had so unceremoniously placed her, almost rigid with fury. 'I'm sick and tired of being shoved around by you!' she cried angrily. 'Who in the *hell* do you think you are?'

'I'm the man who's taking you to his home, ripping off that ridiculously brief, sexy dress, and then making passionate love to you—*that's who I am!*' he ground out harshly through clenched teeth.

As a conversation stopper—it's a winner! she thought hysterically, struck completely dumb as she sat silently beside him while he started the car. Sneaking a quick frightened glance at the hard profile of the man sitting beside her, she simply couldn't seem to think what she was supposed to say or do next. There didn't seem to be any point in shouting and screaming blue murder—because, now they'd left the car park, there was no one around to hear her. And, even if she tried to throw herself out of the car, she'd very likely break a leg—or her neck.

The vehicle roared quickly along a small road, climbing a low hill before speeding down a twisting dirt track which appeared to be leading to the sea. Despite the moon, she could see very little outside the range of the car's headlamps, only the blazing lights of a few large houses, and an occasional cluster of small cottages. All too soon for her peace of mind, Matt brought the car to a screeching halt outside a high brick wall.

Lifting a small black box from the dashboard, he pressed a button. A moment later, a section of the wall appeared to vanish mysteriously, allowing him to drive the car on to a gravelled forecourt in front of a large house.

In the sudden grim, unnerving silence he cut the engine and came around to open her door. And it was only then that Francesca managed to find her tongue at last.

'No! No, Matt, I. . . I must get back to the yacht. . .' she gabbled, flinching at the sight of the harsh, strained expression on his face. Looking desperately around her, she heard him give a heavy, impatient sigh.

'It's lucky you're so slim—because I can see that this is getting to be a habit!' he said with a dry bark of sardonic laughter as he swept her up in his arms.

Ignoring her startled cry of protest, he strode up the

steps and through an arched doorway into an enormously wide marble-floored hall.

Maybe under normal circumstances Francesca might have been interested in her surroundings. But while she was struggling violently in Matt's arms she merely had a confused impression of a light, airy structure as he strode swiftly across the floor towards a large mahogany door. And then, not pausing as he swiftly kicked the door open, Matt carried her into a room and tossed her down on to a deep leather sofa.

Stunned and winded, her blue eyes wide with nervous apprehension and fright, she stared at him in shock as he retraced his steps to the door. The only sound to disturb the ominous silence was the loud click of a key being firmly rotated in the lock, and then he slowly turned around to face her.

Having gazed at the stern, unrelenting expression on his tanned face, Francesca's eyes skidded nervously about the room. There seemed to be no escape from the tall, dark figure leaning so nonchalantly against the locked door. The only other exit from the room was a huge plate-glass window which formed one wall of the large area. But it appeared to be firmly closed against the heat outside—a fact reinforced as she gradually became aware that the room was air-conditioned.

'Please, Matt—this is ridiculous. I. . . I must go back!' she exclaimed, desperately aware of the breathless, unsteady note in her voice as she struggled to swing her legs off the sofa.

'You're not going anywhere.'

The quiet finality of his words was far more frightening than any anger would have been. She could feel her head beginning to throb with the tension, and there seemed nothing she could do to stop herself from trembling almost uncontrollably.

'You. . .you can't keep me here!' she cried, jumping to her feet in agitation.

'Oh—can't I?' he drawled slowly, beginning to move menacingly towards her, the gleam in his determined green eyes carrying an unmistakable message. Backing nervously away from him, she stumbled and bumped into a large table, gasping with pain as the sharp corner of the hard marble top dug into her hip.

It was the last straw.

For goodness knew how many days she'd been under more stress and strain than she'd ever experienced in the whole of her life—other than that time in the South of France eight years ago. And, even then, it had been *Matt* who had been the root cause of all her unhappiness.

Suddenly it all became too much for her to bear any longer. A hard lump seemed to be constricting her throat as Francesca's eyes filled with tears, her slim body racked by sobs as she threw herself down on to a nearby sofa, burying her face in the cushions and weeping as if her heart was broken.

A moment later she heard Matt swearing harshly under his breath, and felt his strong arms closing about her trembling figure.

'Please don't cry, my darling! There's no need for you to weep like this. . .' he murmured soothingly as he gathered her into his warm embrace. Continuing to utter soft, husky endearments, he gently stroked her hair, quietly rocking her in his arms until the flowing torrent of tears began to cease, and she lay exhausted against his chest.

'I. . . I'm s-sorry. . .' she hiccuped. 'I d-don't know what's c-come over me.'

'No. . . I'm the one who should be apologising to you,' he sighed, twisting slightly to remove a handkerchief from his pocket and gently wiping the tears from her face. 'I didn't mean. . . I had no intention of frightening you, darling,' he added softly. 'I was just trying to make sure we could have an uninterrupted talk—something that's been impossible on the yacht.'

'But you s-said. . .you threatened to. . .' She sniffed, her body still shaken by occasional sobs.

'Make love to you? *Of course* I want to make love to you—you silly girl!' His voice rose in exasperation.

'There you go again!' she moaned helplessly, tears filling her eyes once more.

Matt gave a heavy sigh. 'Darling Francesca—what an idiot you are!' he murmured, raising his handkerchief again to wipe her eyes, before covering her upturned face with soft, butterfly-light kisses.

'Now, I want you to stop crying, and listen to me,' he said firmly. And when she gave a slight nod of her head, burying her flushed cheeks in the curve of his broad shoulder, he took a deep breath. 'God knows, we've got a lot to talk about. But let's get one thing clear first of all. I do not—repeat *not*—intend to force myself on you. OK?'

'But in the car you said——'

'I know—and I'm sorry about that.' He shook his dark head in self-disgust. 'All I can say in my own defence is that I've been a desperate man! Although I thought I'd started this whole affair with a stacked deck of cards, every ace I've played has turned out to be a complete dud! And, with the arrival on the scene of that tiresome rogue James Fielding, matters have swiftly gone from bad to worse!'

'Matt, I'm sorry. . .' she raised her head to gaze up at him in bafflement '. . . I don't have the least idea of what you're talking about. I mean. . . I'm not interested in James. . .'

'He's certainly intersted in *you*!' Matt ground out through clenched teeth. 'These last few days I've been sorely tempted to strangle the damned man—and he's lucky not to have been chucked overboard into the sea!'

'You're not the only one who's been sorely tempted—I'd have cheerfully thrown you *both* into the sea,' she retorted bitterly. 'In fact, I'm sick and tired of being treated as a. . .a sex object. Yes, James has been trying to flirt with me—but it was only to wind you up. He knows. . . I know—and I expect the whole of Mustique knows by now!—that you're only interested in getting me into your bed,' she ground out, struggling in his embrace.

'That's not true!' he told her fiercely.

'Oh, no!' She gave a shrill cry of unhappy laughter as she finally tore herself free of his arms, quickly jumping up and spinning around to face him. 'Right from the first moment I arrived out here in the Caribbean you made it absolutely clear that you wanted me. And why you should—when you so clearly think that I'm worthless, and have been treating me as though I were the scum of the earth—I have absolutely *no* idea!'

'Of course I want you!' he growled huskily, swiftly rising to his feet. 'I would be lying if I said otherwise. But that's only part of it.'

'Part of what?' she lashed back angrily. 'The part where I'm expected to cook and scrub on your damn boat? The part when I have to put up with your lousy friends? Or the part where I have to watch you flirting with luscious Lois?'

'Don't be such a damn fool, Francesca!' he exploded savagely, taking a menacing step towards her trembling figure. 'You must be blind, deaf and dumb not to know that I'm madly in love with you!'

CHAPTER NINE

'You're *what*?' Francesca gasped, the wind completely taken out of her sails as she stared up at Matt with dazed eyes. 'Are you really trying to tell me that. . . that. . .?'

'That I'm madly and passionately in love with you?' Matt completed the sentence impatiently. 'Yes, of course I am—you idiot!'

'Oh, great! You certainly sound *very* romantic, I must say!' she muttered sarcastically, still trying to absorb what he'd just said. Maybe he didn't really mean it. Was it yet another of the games he seemed to like to play with other people's emotions? If only she could trust him. . .

Matt gave a shamefaced, rueful bark of laughter. 'Darling one, you're quite right. I'm sorry if I don't sound very lover-like, but it's been an extremely trying few days.' He sighed heavily, pushing a hand through his dark hair. 'However, I can assure you that I do love you, very deeply. And yes, I want to marry you—as soon as I possibly can. The only problem I've got at the moment is to try and find out exactly how *you* feel about me. I. . . I know that I haven't been kind. In fact, I've behaved like a perfect ogre. . .'

'You're so right!'

'. . .but I can explain that. At least, I hope I can,' he

added anxiously, his dark brows creasing into a worried frown as he stared intently down at her.

His darling Francesca, who normally had the most expressive features, making it easy for him to tell exactly what she was thinking, was now regarding him with a dead-pan expression on her lovely face. *Oh, God!*—he hadn't left it too late, had he? Was this wonderful girl going to turn him down? It was no more than he deserved, of course, he thought grimly as he desperately tried to cope with the fact that—for practically the first time in his life—he wasn't in charge of events. There was nothing to stop her walking out of here and out of his life—forever. He *must* try and get her to listen to him. Maybe then he'd have a chance. If he could only get her to trust him. . .

'Look, darling,' he said, putting a hand lightly on her shoulder, 'why don't we both sit down and have a drink while I explain why I've been such a rotten bastard, hmm?'

The effect of his warm, sensual smile was devastating, and it was all Francesca could do not to throw herself into his arms. But hearing him say that he loved her, and that he also wanted to marry her, had given her a new strength. With the centuries-old instinct born into women, she knew that she mustn't give in too easily to him. Knowing Matt, she realised that this was likely to be her only opportunity to have him on the run. And, while she had no intention of humbling this proud man, he certainly owed her a very full explanation of his dreadful behaviour. He'd referred to himself as having been a 'rotten bastard'—and she had no intention of arguing with that description!

'I don't think I'm ready to hear any long explanations just at the moment,' she said coolly, finally breaking the long silence between them. 'But, although I'd like a drink, what I'd really love most of all is to have a bath! Since there was only a small shower available on the yacht, I'm dying to relax in a deep warm bath.'

Although she'd felt well in command of herself—and the situation—Francesca wasn't so sure that she'd made the right decision when, half an hour later, she found herself lying in the scented water of one of the most spacious and sumptuous bathrooms she'd ever seen.

When she'd asked for a bath, Matt had merely raised a dark eyebrow before smoothly informing her that his house and servants were at her disposal. His easy acceptance of her request had left her feeling badly shaken. She'd expected at least *some* argument. For one thing, it was so totally out of character for Matt to allow anyone to dictate terms to him, and for another. . .well, it wasn't at all the reaction that she'd expected. She knew she ought to be ashamed to admit, even to herself, that she'd half expected. . .half wanted. . .what? To have him force himself on her? No, she told herself quickly, that wasn't it. But, all the same, she couldn't help wishing that he'd overruled her request, that he'd demonstrated his usual masterful command of himself and the situation. . .

Telling herself not to be so ridiculous, Francesca tried to concentrate on her surroundings. Not only was this an amazing bathroom—with a hot tub, jacuzzi, two shower stalls and at least two of everything else!—but what she'd seen of the house was equally luxurious.

When he'd unlocked the sitting-room door, and rung for his housekeeper, Matt had explained that he had deliberately designed a very private hideaway for himself on Mustique. 'You can imagine my consternation when dear Gloria insisted on staying on the island,' he'd told her with a rueful smile. 'I'd been hoping to leave everyone on the yacht in Bequia—and then sail back here with you.' However, the arrival of the housekeeper—a fat, smiling, middle-aged woman, whom he'd introduced as Calvin's wife, Phoebe—had prevented her from learning any more.

Phoebe had been very warm, friendly and extremely helpful. After showing Francesca into a large, airy, beautifully decorated bedroom, with its *en-suite* bathroom and dressing-rooms, she'd hurried away to return a few minutes later with a white towelling robe. 'Mr Sinclair keeps some of these by the pool for his friends,' she'd told the girl. 'But he ain't had any young ladies staying here before now, and so I guess you is plumb out of luck if you needs anything else!'

Knowing that she wasn't the latest in a long line of girlfriends who'd stayed in his house had proved to be a soothing balm to her troubled spirit. As had been the opportunity to take off the silver sequinned dress, which she wished to goodness she'd never decided to put on tonight. The garish garment—just possibly acceptable for a fun evening, dancing under the stars—had made her look flashy and vulgar within the cool, sophisticated setting of Matt's large sitting-room.

However, it was no good putting off the evil hour, she told herself, reluctantly stepping out of the bath and towelling herself dry. Wrapping herself in the short towelling robe, she made her way back into the bedroom. Lamps glowed beside the ornately ruched mosquito-netting draped over the large four-poster bed, throwing a soft light on the white walls and smooth marble flooring that was so refreshingly cool to the feet. Still feeling hot and flushed from her bath, she drifted across the floor to where the white muslin curtains over the open french windows rustled in the soft evening breeze.

The glass doors opened on to what appeared to be a large patio, which ran the length of the house, overlooking the beach and the ocean. The moonlight streamed down on to the terracotta tubs of flowering shrubs and the exuberant, waving fronds of bougainvillaea, their vivid colours bleached into monochrome by the startlingly clear, eerie light.

As she stood motionless in the doorway her eyes were irresistibly drawn to the tall figure of Matt, standing with his back to her as he gazed out over the ocean. Like her, he must have felt the need of a bath or shower, since his tall frame was covered only by a short towel draped around his waist. Her heart seemed to leap in her body as an unbearable longing surged through her limbs. Her mouth seemed suddenly dry and her body was rocked by a convulsive wave of sensuality, which left her shaken and trembling as she fought an overwhelming urge to run and put her arms about him.

The small gasp which escaped her lips alerted him to her presence. Slowly turning around to look at the girl standing between the open windows, his green eyes swept over the cloud of silvery-white ash-blonde hair flowing down over her shoulders, her long tanned legs beneath the short robe whose belt tightly clasped her slim waist.

And then. . .as Matt walked slowly and silently towards her. . .then it seemed that she was somehow taking part in the shadowy erotic dream which had repeated itself so often during the past eight years— and which had returned with such startling clarity on the night of her arrival in Grenada. Once again, as in the dream, she was unable to move as he drew nearer, her eyes locked with his as he raised his hands and placed them gently on her shoulders.

'Francesca. . .?'

The low, husky note in his voice seemed to be coming from far away as his hands skimmed lightly down over her quivering figure to undo her belt. And then she could feel the cool touch of his fingers on her heated body as the robe fell about her feet.

'*Francesca!*' She heard his hoarse cry, but as the hard pressure of his mouth sought the parted, trembling sweetness of her lips all coherent thought was obliterated and he crushed her firmly to his bare chest. Her heightened senses were assailed by the aromatic tang of his cologne, the warmth of his body, and the heavy pounding of his heart beating loudly in unison with her own. As his kiss deepened, excitement zigzagged like lightning through her trembling body, shocking her out of her dream-world and into the present.

Matt raised his head, his breathing as ragged and unsteady as her own, the blazing, feverish glitter in his eyes causing her almost to faint with a tremulous, aching need for his possession.

'Oh, my darling! I love you so much—and I've been such a *fool* all these years!' The tortured savagery in his voice seemed to cut her to the heart, and she slid her arms up about his neck, her fingers burying themselves in his dark hair as she pulled him closer to her warm, melting body.

Moments later, she found herself swept up into his arms and swiftly carried towards the bed. As his arms closed about her naked figure once more, the musky male scent of him aroused her almost unbearably. She pressed her lips to his chest, relishing the heat of his skin, the strength of the muscles clenching convulsively beneath the soft caress of her mouth. His skin felt so smooth beneath her fingertips, warm and velvety as her hands moved exploratively over his body.

Her action provoked a deep growl from his throat. Quickly discarding the brief towel he'd been wearing, he leaned over her, his hands cupping the full softness of her firm breasts. She gasped at the touch of his lips moving caressingly over her warm flesh, moaning helplessly at the raw heat of his mouth against her aching, swollen nipples.

She had no experience to guide her, only an instinctive need and desire for his possession. Arching her body against him, she was barely aware that her eager response to his lovemaking could be fragmenting his self-control. There seemed nothing more important than that Matt continue to stroke, caress and kiss her body. . .nothing more she desired than to seek fulfilment and satisfaction from the urgent, throbbing excitement which seemed to have her in thrall.

'Dear God—I've wanted you for so long!' he

breathed, his voice husky and thick with passion as his lovemaking became more urgent, more arousing. Her senses spinning in a frenzy of delight beneath the mastery of his touch, she cried out with both the sharp, sudden pain and then with ecstasy as the hard thrusting strength of his manhood possessed her. And then her last conscious thought was that she was drowning. . .drowning in a vast storm of passion as waves of feverish convulsions shook her body, culminating in a brilliant firework explosion of mutual fulfilment and pleasure.

Francesca opened her eyes the next morning to find herself alone in the huge bed. Smiling as she lay back on the pillows, she stretched her languorous, satiated body. Her cheeks flushed as she looked down at her naked figure beneath the crumpled sheet, recalling how, twice before dawn, Matt's light but insistent touch had aroused her, and how ardently and eagerly she had responded to his passionate lovemaking.

Not having worn her watch last night, she had no idea of the time. However, deciding that she couldn't stay in bed all day, she got up to have a shower. It was only when she was drying herself, and wondering what she was going to wear, that she began to think about the reality of her situation. Matt had said he loved her, and that he wanted to marry her. But, despite the storm of passion which had engulfed them, there still remained so many questions to be answered. Sinking slowly down on to the edge of the bed, she felt weighed down by the heavy burden of her complicated relationship with Matt, which had plagued and tormented her for so long.

Slipping on the towelling robe and belting it tightly around her slender waist, she wandered through the house, which appeared to be deserted. Where was Matt? she wondered, beginning to feel increasingly awkward and unsure of herself. The fresh morning sunshine tempted her nervous figure out on to the patio, and then, looking across the silver sand towards the sea, she saw Matt's tall figure walking slowly along the water's edge.

By the time she reached him, he was sitting on a rock and gazing out to sea. Hesitating for a moment, she placed a tentative hand on his shoulder.

'Matt?' She felt his powerful shoulders rise and fall as he gave a long-drawn-out, heavy sigh.

'Why didn't you tell me?' he demanded, his voice sounding tired and weary as he continued to stare at the waves beating on the shore.

'Tell you—what?'

'That you'd never been to bed with anyone, before last night,' he replied, his voice heavy with bitter self-contempt. 'After all I've done to you—to discover that you were a virgin is just about the last nail in my coffin!'

'It doesn't matter—it's not important!' she cried, impulsively throwing her arms about his unhappy figure.

'Of course it matters—and it *is* important,' he retorted tersely, pulling her down on to his lap and burying his face in the fragrant cloud of her hair. 'You'd only been out here in the Caribbean a few days before I realised that I'd been a blind fool all these years. But even I didn't realise—until last night—*just* what a fool I've been,' he added heavily.

'Oh, for heaven's sake—do stop going on about my virginity!' she told him, her cheeks pink with embarrassment. 'In fact—I'm extremely relieved to be now part of the normal human race. Quite honestly, if any of my friends knew that I'd reached the age of twenty-four without having been to bed with a man, they'd have thought I was *most* peculiar—a real psychiatric case!'

'But. . .'

'Please, Matt—can we drop the subject?' she begged with loving exasperation. 'We've got far more important things to talk about. Such as why you insisted on my cooking for the Wagners on *Silver Lady*. It was a set-up, wasn't it?'

Matt sighed. 'Yes, I'm afraid it was,' he admitted, hesitating for a moment before adding in a low voice, 'I think I must have been temporarily out of my mind. I *think* I wanted you to be as unhappy and miserable as I was—*God knows* what I really wanted, darling,' he groaned. 'To have mentally cracked the whip and treated you like dirt. . Oh, yes, you were quite right, I did. I was a *total bastard*!' he added bitterly, his arms tightening convulsively about her.

'It all seemed to start about the time of my mother's illness and death. I loved her very dearly, and when your father contacted me in the States to tell me about the news I'd just had that traumatic confrontation with Natalie.' He shrugged his shoulders unhappily. 'It wasn't all Natalie's fault, of course. You were quite right—even though she was so much older than me, she was still stunningly beautiful. But when I discovered who she was I. . . I felt utterly disgusted with both her *and* myself.'

'Darling, there's no point in reproaching yourself,' Francesca murmured, raising a hand to brush a lock of his dark hair from his eyes. 'It was obviously one of those ghastly coincidences that occasionally happen in life.'

'You may be right.' He grimaced. 'But it doesn't make it any easier to bear, and at the time I was in quite a state about it. On top of that, I had my mother's illness, which I knew to be terminal—and then. . .then I discovered that you, whom I'd always thought of as a sweet little sister, had become some sort of promiscuous little tart!'

'But I wasn't!' she cried. 'It was that serpent Paula who——'

'Hush, darling,' he murmured soothingly, gently and tenderly stroking the agitated figure in his arms. 'Long afterwards I read about Paula in the papers—she'd been involved in some drug bust. But at the time, I must tell you, she was very plausible. Of course I wanted to believe you, but I had considerable difficulty in coping with the fact that you *weren't* a sweet, shy little girl any more. You were almost a grown woman— and a highly desirable one at that!

'So, I'd nearly been seduced by Natalie; learned that my mother was dying; and thought I'd discovered that you were a tramp—all in the space of a few weeks!' He shook his dark head at the distressing memories of the past. 'To crown it all, and what turned the whole mess into explosive dynamite, was the shaming fact that—

somehow—I seemed to have fallen in love with my little stepsister, who wasn't even sixteen!'

'Maybe if you hadn't had all those other problems your feelings for me would have died a natural death,' Francesca said slowly.

'No chance!' he said firmly. 'I knew what I felt for you wasn't a passing phase. I wanted to possess you body and soul, even then. Even if you'd been innocent of Paula's charges—and I really did try very hard to believe that you were—I wanted you with a fierce longing that almost tore me apart. At the same time I utterly despised myself for lusting after someone who was still, in many ways, a child. That terrible night, after my mother's funeral, when you so innocently offered yourself to me. . .' He swallowed and took a deep breath. 'Dear God—I don't think I'll ever forget it!'

'But it's all over now,' she murmured softly. 'We've found each other once again. And we're both so much wiser now.'

'You would think so, wouldn't you?' He gave a caustic laugh. 'Darling, I don't expect you to understand—because I'm not sure that even *I* do—but for the past eight years your silvery shadow has trailed such a dark, destructive path through my life that when fate seemed to place you very neatly in my hands—and at my mercy—I didn't hesitate. I was determined to exorcise your ghost, once and for all! I'd been keeping tabs on you, of course, and when I learned that that chinless wonder you worked with had moved into your apartment—that was *it*!'

'Oh, Matt—you really *are* an idiot!' She gave a

nervous giggle. 'Rupert isn't interested in *women*! And he only borrowed a room in my flat while his own place was being redecorated.'

'Hmm. . .yes, well, it would appear that I seem to have slipped up there.' He gave her a shamefaced grin. 'But I didn't know that at the time, did I? You appeared to be living openly with a man—and I wasn't prepared to stand for it! But I knew that you needed money for the art gallery, and that you'd eventually have to come to me for it. . .as, indeed, you did.'

Francesca grimaced. 'I tried every other avenue I could think of, but no one would lend me that amount of money. So I had to contact you in the end—and I dreaded having to come out here with a begging-bowl in my hand.'

'And I was ready for you,' he told her heavily. 'Ben had arranged, a long time ago, to join me for a cruise around the Windward Islands. All I had to do was to make up a reason for needing you as a cook and invite his awful wife and daughter along. I'd known them for some time, and I could guarantee that the two women would make your life a misery.'

'Lois is very beautiful,' Francesca said in a small voice.

'Yes, she is, isn't she?' Matt agreed calmly. 'However, the girl is also a first-class, empty-headed, spoilt nincompoop! I've never been so insulted in my life as when you accused me of wanting to marry the silly girl!' he added, gazing down at her with a sardonic grin.

'Well—it was clear she wanted to marry *you*!' Francesca retorted huffily. 'In fact, when I think about the hundreds of women you must have had, I really don't——'

'Now—just a minute!' he said firmly. 'I'm not in the first flush of youth—and I'm not going to pretend that I've been living like a monk. However, I give you my solemn promise that, since you captured my heart eight years ago, I've had only light, easy relationships with women who didn't want to become involved in a serious affair any more than I did. OK?'

'Yes,' she sighed. 'I'll try not to be jealous.'

'You have no need to be. I love you with all my heart,' he told her simply. 'I experienced total ecstasy and joy in your arms last night. And, since we made love I don't know how many times. . .'

'Three,' she answered quickly, before flushing a deep crimson as he gave a low, sensual laugh.

'. . . I think you can rest assured that I am *not* in the slightest bit interested in anyone else! And, incidentally, I'm still waiting to hear if you're going to marry me,' he added, his arms tightening about her possessively.

'Well, I think you ought to make an honest woman of me, don't you?' She smiled up at him.

'Absolutely!' he agreed. 'I'm sure I can arrange a marriage licence here on Mustique, and we can hold the reception at Silver Beach.'

She frowned. 'Where's that?'

'This house, of course,' he said. 'And then, how about a honeymoon on the yacht, and——'

'Hold it!' she said quickly. 'What about the art gallery? I'd got to the point, lately, when I wished I'd never thought of trying to buy the place.'

'Well, that's one thing you don't have to worry about,' he told her with a grin. 'I bought it for you—with my own money, of course—before we started to cruise around the islands on *Silver Lady*. I think it must be the only thing that I did right during the whole time you've been in the Caribbean,' he added gloomily.

'But I can't run the gallery and be married to you at one and the same time,' she told him with a worried frown. 'Quite honestly, Matt, I think you'd better sell the art gallery.'

'Oh, no—Ben was quite right. It's a very good investment. I suggest that you put in a manager, and we will think about what to do with it in a year or two's time.'

'Well, there is one more thing. You do remember what I said about the yo-ho-ho life on the ocean wave, don't you? I'm not saying that I'm always going to be anti-sailing, but I do think I've had enough of the sea—for the time being!'

'Fair enough—how about wild-game spotting in Kenya instead?'

'That sounds great!' she beamed up at him.

'Although I think you aren't giving yourself sufficient credit,' he told her seriously. 'The way you tore into cleaning up the yacht, and managed to cope with such an alien environment, was what helped to make the scales fall from my eyes; to realise just how I had maligned you all these years. You were frightened and terrified of the sea, and yet you managed to stay on your feet, looking after everyone when they had completely lost their nerve. Not only was I deeply ashamed of my own behaviour in trying to make your life as unhappy as I could,' he added sorrowfully, 'but I was *very* proud of you.'

Francesca's cheeks flushed at his praise. 'There is just one thing. . .' she murmured. 'It's not very important really, but I don't quite understand why you seem to have this obsession for "silver". There's this house of yours, Silver Beach, and the yacht *Silver Lady*. Is it something to do with your business, or——?'

She didn't manage to finish the sentence, as he gave a deep, throaty chuckle.

'I was so certain that you must have guessed—but it isn't easy to change the name of a boat. However, since you clearly haven't realised the connection. . .' He raised his hand to pick up a lock of her silvery ash-blonde hair.

'You, my darling, have always been my one and only silver lady,' he said softly, before lowering his head to possess her lips in a lingering kiss of aching sweetness and total commitment.

HARLEQUIN®

PRESENTS® *plus*

Meet Lily Norfolk. Not even her husband's tragic death can convince her to tell his brother, Dane Norfolk, the truth behind their marriage. It's better that he believe she married Daniel for his money and that she had an affair with Daniel's best friend. It's better that Dane keep his distance!

And then there's Elizabeth. She's a respectable young woman, but she also has a secret mission and a secret repressed sensual side. Jake Hawkwood's never liked secrets—he's determined to uncover everything Elizabeth's been hiding....

Lily and Elizabeth are just two of the passionate women you'll discover each month in Harlequin Presents Plus. And if you think they're passionate, wait until you meet Dane and Jake!

Watch for
HOUSE OF GLASS by Michelle Reid
Harlequin Presents Plus #1615
and
THE HAWK AND THE LAMB by Susan Napier
Harlequin Presents Plus #1616

Harlequin Presents Plus
The best has just gotten better!

Available in January wherever Harlequin Books are sold.

**Fifty red-blooded, white-hot, true-blue hunks
from every State in the Union!**

Look for MEN MADE IN AMERICA! Written by some
of our most poplar authors, these stories feature fifty of
the strongest, sexiest men, each from a different state in
the union!

Two titles available every other month at your favorite
retail outlet.

In January, look for:

DREAM COME TRUE by Ann Major (Florida)
WAY OF THE WILLOW by Linda Shaw (Georgia)

In March, look for:

TANGLED LIES by Anne Stuart (Hawaii)
ROGUE'S VALLEY by Kathleen Creighton (Idaho)

You won't be able to resist MEN MADE IN AMERICA!

POSTCARDS FROM EUROPE

HARLEQUIN PRESENTS®

Hi!
Spending a year in Europe. You won't believe how great the men are! Will be visiting Greece, Italy, France and more.

Wish you were here—how about joining us in January?

There's a handsome Greek just waiting to meet you.

THE ALPHA MAN
by Kay Thorpe

Harlequin Presents #1619

Available in January wherever Harlequin books are sold.

HPPFEG